"You're angry, aren't you?" Kendra whispered. *"I can feel it in you. Why are you so angry?"*

"I'm not angry," Joel denied quickly, knowing that he wasn't telling the truth. "It's just that I don't like my reaction to a woman to be quite this violent. You know that what's happening between us couldn't be considered ordinary."

"Yes," she answered dreamily. "You have a lovely mouth, do you know that?" Her index finger reached up to trace the sensual line of his lower lip. It was smooth and warm beneath her finger and she felt a breathless tingle. His lips parted suddenly to capture her finger, and for the briefest instant she felt the nip of his teeth before he released it.

"The better to eat you with," he said lightly, but the pulse in his neck was throbbing wildly and his cheeks were flushed. "You're a feast that would tempt the gods, sweetheart, and I find I'm a very hungry man . . ."

WHAT ARE *LOVESWEPT* ROMANCES?

They are stories of true romance and touching emotion. We believe those two very important ingredients are constants in our highly sensual and very believable stories in the *LOVESWEPT* line. Our goal is to give you, the reader, stories of consistently high quality that may sometimes make you laugh, sometimes make you cry, but are always fresh and creative and contain many delightful surprises within their pages.

Most romance fans read an enormous number of books. Those they truly love, they keep. Others may be traded with friends and soon forgotten. We hope that each *LOVESWEPT* romance will be a treasure—a "keeper." We will always try to publish

LOVE STORIES YOU'LL NEVER FORGET
BY AUTHORS YOU'LL ALWAYS REMEMBER

The Editors

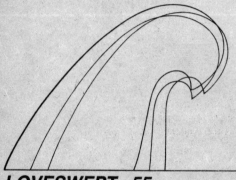

LOVESWEPT • 55

Iris Johansen
Capture The Rainbow

BANTAM BOOKS

TORONTO • NEW YORK • LONDON • SYDNEY • AUCKLAND

CAPTURE THE RAINBOW

A Bantam Book / August 1984

ISBN 0-553-21664-3

Published simultaneously in the United States and Canada

*Bantam Books are published by Bantam Books, Inc. Its
trademark, consisting of the words "Bantam Books" and the
portrayal of a rooster, is Registered in U.S. Patent and Trademark Office and in other countries. Marca Registrada. Bantam
Books, Inc., 666 Fifth Avenue, New York, New York 10103.*

PRINTED IN THE UNITED STATES OF AMERICA

O   0 9 8 7 6 5 4 3 2 1

One

His cynical face had the wicked fascination of a fallen angel and he had the strange olive-green eyes of a sorcerer capable of conjuring both white *and* black magic.

As Kendra's gaze met his across the crowded room, she felt a queer breathless shock and her hand tightened involuntarily on the stem of her cocktail glass. There was a mesmerizing intensity about those deep-set eyes; she felt as though she was wrapped in a shimmering force field of power. And suddenly she felt weak and ineffectual. Then one of the men in the little coterie surrounding Damon spoke to him and he glanced away, releasing her.

Releasing? Good heavens, she was being fanciful tonight! She made a conscious effort to relax her death grip on her glass.

She must be more tired than she realized. Joel Damon might be known for being something of a miracle worker as a director, but there was nothing in the least supernatural about him personally. His reputation with women was scandalous, even in the permissive culture of Tinsel Town. That narrowed, searing glance he had directed at her had merely been the appraisal of a virile predator seeking new prey. She surely should be used to that by now.

Her hand absently rubbed at the nagging little pain in the small of her back. The moment she became aware of what she was doing, she quickly jerked her hand away. This must be her night for being stupid. There were too many people here who would recognize and correctly interpret that little sign of weakness for exactly what it was. That had to be avoided at all costs. All she had to do was hold on until the painkiller she'd taken fifteen minutes earlier had time to take effect; then she'd be fine. The gag today had been rough and she was tired—that's why the ache seemed so unbearable at the moment.

"God, you look gorgeous, Ken," Dave Balding's voice was lazily admiring her as he appeared at her side.

He looked more like an ebullient genie than ever, she thought. Oh, dear, yet another mythical simile. Her lips turned up in a rueful smile. "So do you, Dave," she said lightly. "I don't think I've ever seen you in a tuxedo. You look quite dashing."

He made a face. "Come on, Ken, cut the bull. We've known each other too long for me to swallow that." His blue eyes were twinkling as he patted his slightly rotund stomach. "Even Sheila said I looked like a pregnant penguin in all this sartorial glory. She should know; she's due herself next month."

"Is Shelia here?" Kendra's gaze eagerly searched the room, but Dave was shaking his head.

"Nope." He lifted his glass to his lips. "She

didn't feel up to this kind of bash tonight. You know how she is when she's pregnant. She gets positively claustrophobic in crowds." He frowned. "I didn't like leaving her alone, but I couldn't risk offending the great man." He gestured mockingly toward Joel Damon across the room. "I may be assistant producer, but that doesn't mean I don't jump when Damon whistles. I have instructions from Michael Donovan that he's to have everything he wants for *Desert Venture.*"

Kendra's brows lifted in surprise. Michael Donovan of Donovan, Ltd. Productions didn't have the reputation of relinquishing one iota of his power as executive producer in the blockbuster hits his company produced. Though he gave his directors complete artistic license, his iron hand was always visible behind the scenes. "That's rather unusual, isn't it?"

Dave nodded. "I'll say it is." He took a sip of his drink. "But then, so is Joel Damon. He can write his own ticket with any film studio in Hollywood these days. He picked up his second Oscar last year, you know."

"How could I help it?" With an odd sense of reluctance her gaze followed his to the corner of the room. In the conventional tuxedo he wore with such careless elegance, Damon's tall slim body gave off an aura of power that dominated the little circle around him. There was a lazy smile on those cynical lips now as he looked down at the woman beside him. She was chattering with almost desperate vivacity in the attempt to hold his attention. His green sorcerer's eyes were nearly hidden by his heavy lids, so that only a jewel-bright gleam shone through the dark lashes. Then those lashes flicked up and his gaze met hers with the impact of an electric shock. Electricity. Yes, that was the word for the whorls of power that were radiating from him, and again she was conscious of the sensation of being caught in the paws of a predator.

This time his oddly possessive glance didn't stop at her face, but wandered over her golden throat and shoulders to the full thrust of her breasts against the cinnamon chiffon gown. His gaze lingered there for a long moment and, incredibly, she felt her breasts respond to his hot glance as if he actually touched her. Then he looked at her slim waist, hips, and long legs. When his glance shifted from her to Dave, she let out her breath in a rush of relief.

Dave Balding's lips pursed in a soundless whistle. "When did you meet Joel Damon, Ken? I have an idea you didn't need my help to get you on the payroll."

"What?" She shook her head as if to clear it. What in heaven's name was wrong with her tonight? "I've never met the man," she said lightly. "I imagine the only reason I was invited to this party was that his secretary noticed my name on the production log." Her glance flitted around the room, dramatically decorated in black and white. "It's far from a select gathering anyway. Everyone from the wardrobe woman to the key grip is here tonight." Her gaze returned to the blonde standing beside Damon. "Not to mention half the starlets in Hollywood."

"Joel's leaving for Sedikhan tomorrow and he usually throws a party for the cast and crew the night before he goes on location," Dave said. "Not that I think he enjoys it. I get the distinct impression that the social scene bores him to tears." He moved his shoulders uneasily. "You're sure you haven't met him before? That look I'm getting from our lord and master is definitely menacing."

"It has to be your imagination," She said deliberately, shifting her position so that her back was turned to Damon. But even then she could feel the force of his gaze on her bare back and shoulders. "From what I've heard, it's not unusual for Joel Damon to display an interest in a woman. Any woman." She took several sips of her champagne before speaking again. "Perhaps his boredom is extending to that lush little blonde who's hanging on to his every word."

"Maybe." Dave's smile brightened his plain face. "It's not the first time you've shut out the competition without even trying." His admiring glance skimmed over her long chestnut hair. It tumbled down her back in a silken curtain and shimmered with a thousand tiny flames in the softly lit room. "Most men take one look at you and immediately decide that you're just what they need as an erotic nightcap. I don't know how I escaped your luscious allure all these years."

"I do." Kendra's deep brown eyes were twinkling. "It probably had something to do with the fact that I tagged after you and Casey from the time I could toddle. What's that expression—'familiarity breeds contempt'?"

His face sobered. "Never contempt, Kendra," he said quietly, raising his hand and gently stroking the curve of her cheek. "I think I respect you more than anyone I've ever known." He hesitated. "How is Casey?"

"Better," she answered. "Much better." Her face clouded. "He was pretty bitter at first, but who could blame him? I don't think anyone could accept being partially paralyzed without going a little crazy. Particularly a man like Casey who knew it also meant the end of his career as a stuntman." She tried to smile. "He's studying law now, you know. Casey always was a great one for talking. He'll probably become a Supreme Court justice before he's satisfied."

"I wouldn't doubt it," Dave said softly. "Casey's the type of man who gets whatever he goes after. Is he still in that convalescent home in the Valley?"

She nodded. "Dr. Dystron says he'll be there at least for another six months for physical therapy. He's really chomping at the bit to get back to the real world." Her lips tightened with determination. "But I'll be damned if I'll let him get out before he can get around without that walker. It's going to be tough enough for him facing all of his old friends in the business. Besides, he'd start skipping the outpatient therapy; and he needs all those nurses right there to nag him about it."

Dave's eyes were thoughtful. "You know, when we were all kids together, you were the quiet gentle one who let Casey and me stampede all over you. It seemed impossible sometimes that you were really brother and sister." His hand moved from her cheek to squeeze her shoulder affectionately. "Somewhere along the way you've managed to develop into one hell of a woman, Ken."

"I've just grown up," she said simply. "After Casey's accident I didn't have much choice; I had to be strong enough for both of us. Casey needed an adult to depend on, not a child."

"You were only nineteen when Casey broke those vertebrae in his back." Dave's lips tightened. "There should have been someone there to help you. You've gone through hell with those three operations and Casey in one hospital after another." He frowned. "We all wanted to help, Ken. Why wouldn't you let us?"

"What could anyone do?" she asked wearily, her hand rubbing unconsciously at the tendons in the small of her back. "His friends all stood by him. His hospital room looked like a De Mille crowd scene most of the time. You were all wonderful to support him like that. The rest was my responsibility." She smiled up at him. "But you all helped there, too. You got me the stunts to help pay all those medical bills." She made a face. "Well, almost all the bills. The operations have been paid for now; that leaves only the convalescent home to worry about."

"I don't know if we did you any favors doing that." His concerned gaze was on the hand rubbing her back. "You've been overdoing it, Ken. All the stunt boys say so. You've been taking any job that comes along and not insisting on proper safety measures. I heard you tore up some tendons in your back a few months ago, yet you were back on the set six weeks later. Is your back is still bothering you?"

She dropped her hand away quickly. "No, not at all," she lied. "I'm just a little stiff because of a fall I took from a horse this afternoon. The stunt coordinator misjudged the spot where I'd fall and dug up the earth three feet from the place the lariat actually toppled me off my trusty steed."

"You're lucky you didn't break any bones," he said grimly. "Like I said, you're not being careful enough in choosing your jobs. The wrong stunt coordinator can get a person killed. I bet you didn't even insist on a run-through before the scene was shot."

"The director was in a hurry to finish the day's shooting. He didn't want to take the time." She smiled bitterly. "Time is money, you know. Casey didn't have a run-through either or he might not have skidded that car into a stone wall."

"You should have learned from his mistake," Dave said. "If you're not careful, you'll end up in the hospital yourself and then how will you help Casey?"

"If you want work in this business, you don't argue with the director," she said softly. "You know that as well as I do, Dave. All a stuntwoman needs to get blacklisted is a reputation for not being 'cooperative.' There are too many amateurs out there ready to step in and take the risks just to get the chance to break into the business."

"It's not worth your life, Kendra," Dave said bluntly. "Hell, it's not even that the job really appeals to you. You never did get the kick out of it Casey did."

"But I'm good at it." Kendra smiled gently. "And that's what's important right now. Even as a favor you wouldn't have hired me for *Venture* if I wasn't a competent professional. And you don't have to worry about the stunt coordinator on this picture. Skip Lowden is the best in the business. I've worked for him before."

"He's going to have to be," Dave said. "*Venture* is going to have more stunts than a James Bond thriller. Joel insisted I get the top people in the field." He glanced down at her glass. "You need a refill; shall I get you one?"

"Please." She watched as Dave dodged his way through the crowd to the bar at the end of the room. She seldom had more than one drink, but she had an idea she might need all the help she could get to see her through the evening. Why weren't those damn pills taking effect? Cold fear surged through her. Oh Lord, had the fall damaged the scar tissue on the tendons again? Oh, please, God, not now! She needed this job. She hadn't been entirely truthful with Dave. There had been no need to worry him any more than he was already. Why burden him with the knowledge that she still owed another ten thousand for Casey's last operation and that the convalescent home bills were astronomical?

"Dave told me you were on the team, but I wasn't sure you'd be here tonight." The southwestern drawl was unmistakable, so was the lean hard-bitten face of the man who appeared at her side. Skip Lowden was in his early forties, but the only thing that testified to his age was a sprinkling of gray at his temples. The rest of him was all tough whipcord muscle and cool coordinated power. A power that was echoed in the keen razor-sharp gray eyes gazing into her own. "I heard you took a little tumble this afternoon."

She should have known he would have heard, she thought in resignation. The professional stuntworld was a very tight network and Skip was prominent in the hierarchy. "It wasn't much," she said defensively. "We got it on the second take."

"The second take should have been the first!" His voice resonated with authority. "You should have insisted on a run-through. Particularly with an amateurish ass like Bodine running the show. You know better than that, Ken."

She was getting very tired of hearing that. It was all very well for Skip to talk. He had the experience and reputation to be able to demand . . . and get anything he wanted.

"I'll remember that on *Venture*," she said lightly. "But then, you wouldn't let me run even one risk without planning it out to the last detail. I know the way you work, Skip. I hear I'm to double for the supporting actress, Billie Callahan." A tiny frown wrinkled her brow. "I don't think I've ever heard of her."

"It's her first picture," Skip answered. "She's Joel Damon's new discovery. Brenna Donovan's starring, but the ingenue gets all the stunts." His glance went over her objectively. "You're about the same height, but you'll have to bind your breasts. Billie isn't nearly as . . . voluptuous."

She grimaced. "Not many women are," she said gloomily. "Which is a distinct disadvantage when it comes to doubling for men as well as women. The only place I can get away with it is in a car chase." She gazed up at him, her brown eyes narrowing. "I hear there's a special stunt involving a jeep jumping a canyon in the picture. Is it a big money gag?"

"Eight thousand."

Eight thousand. Together with what she was making for the rest of the picture, it would be almost enough to clear the debt on Casey's operation. "I want it, Skip," she said, her voice vibrating with intensity. "I *need* it."

"I haven't decided who'll do it yet." Skip's voice was as coolly measured as a metronome. "There are five men on the team who have the experience for the job and they'd all give their union cards to get it."

"I could do it. You *know* I could do it. I'm good with cars. Almost as good as Casey was. Give me the gag and you won't be sorry, Skip. I won't let you down. One take, I promise."

"There wouldn't be any question of that," he answered. "There's no run-through possible on this one. It's either make it or end up at the bottom of the canyon. And my people don't end up like Casey, Ken. Not when I'm running the action."

She was still looking at him hopefully, but he was shaking his head. "I'm not going to promise it to you, Ken. I haven't worked with you in two years and I've been hearing a few disturbing things about you lately." He was turning away. "I'll think about it, but I'm not going to commit myself to anything until I watch you work. We'll talk again in Sedikhan."

He was gone as quickly as he'd appeared, leaving her to gaze after him. Disappointment mixed with a glimmer of hope. At least he hadn't rejected the idea entirely and that was something. If he hadn't given the gag to someone else there was still a chance for her to get it. Skip was absolutely fair and, if she could prove herself to him, he'd give her the job.

"Sorry to be so long; the bar was a mob scene." Dave pressed a champagne glass into her hand and grinned down at her. "I saw Skip talking to you so I didn't try to speed up the bartender. I thought you'd welcome the chance to try to get him to let you do the jump. Did you convince him?"

A little smile tugged at her lips. "You know me too well, Dave." She shook her head. "No, he's reserving judgment at the moment, but I'm not giving up."

"I didn't think you would." Dave gave a mock shudder. "Better you than me. That stunt would make Evel Knievil turn pale. I can't understand why you stunt people fight so ferociously for the privilege of breaking your necks."

"Money," she said succinctly. "And the chance of beating a record set by some other stunt person." She took a sip of champagne. "And some can't resist the challenge of walking that tightrope between life and death." She shrugged. "There's any number of reasons why we do it if you think about it."

"None of which makes any sense to a sane individual," Dave said dryly. His blue gaze was fixed musingly on her face. "You appear to be feeling better. There's some color in your cheeks now. When I first saw you, you looked so strained and exhausted that I was worried."

She *was* feeling better, she discovered to her amazement. The painkillers must have done their stuff because her back wasn't aching at all now. In fact, she'd never felt more vibrantly, glowingly alive in her entire life. She looked down at the champagne in her glass and smiled broadly. She felt like one of the bubbles that rose in the golden liquid—effervescent, yet very clear and sharp. It was such a lovely sensation. But was it too lovely? She couldn't be a little tipsy, could she?

Nonsense, she had only had one glass of champagne! It must be the relief of knowing she had a chance at the jump that explained this strange exhilaration. "I feel fine," she said, smiling brilliantly at Dave. "Wonderful. Now why don't you tell me what you and Sheila have been up to lately?"

She continued to float on iridescent bubbles during the next hour and, if possible, the euphoria escalated to an even more shimmering plateau. When she'd first arrived at Joel Damon's home in Laurel Canyon, she had thought the stark black-and-white decor was cold. Now she changed her mind. It was a perfectly beautiful room. Everything was perfectly beautiful.

Dave's face was beautiful too, with his bright blue eyes and warm understanding smile. But he wasn't smiling at the moment, she realized hazily.

"Are you okay, Ken?" Dave's voice was full of concern.

She looked at him wonderingly. What a foolish question. "Of course I am," she said liltingly. "I was a little tired before, but now I've got my second wind."

His glance dropped speculatively to her glass. "I have an idea that's not all you've got. How many cocktails did you have before I found you in this mob?"

Did he think she was tipsy? The idea was so absurd that her throaty laugh rang out causing a few bystanders to look at her in surprise. "Only one," she answered, standing on her tiptoes to plant an affectionate kiss on his cheek. "You know I never have more than two in an evening."

"I thought I did." He frowned as he studied her

flushed cheeks and velvet-brown eyes shining with an almost feverish excitement. He linked his arms loosely about her waist. "But something's sure got you lit up like neon. Are you on something?"

"On something?"

"Coke, uppers, Quaaludes?" he enumerated tersely.

"Don't be silly," she said indignantly. "I've seen enough careers blown to atoms by drugs to shy away from them like the plague." Drugs. She had taken that painkiller earlier but it could have no connection with this lovely mood she was in. Well, perhaps a minor connection. It had taken the pain away and no doubt relief was partly responsible for the joyous ebullience that was surging through her. But she wasn't going to worry about that now. She was too happy. It seemed a lifetime since she'd felt this irresponsible, this free from care.

"I think I'd better take you home." Clearly worried, Dave chewed at his lower lip. "Where's your wrap?"

"I think one of the maids put it in a bedroom upstairs," she said vaguely. "But I can't go home yet. I haven't paid my respects to the wizard. He might get angry and turn me into a frog." She shook her head, her forehead knitting in thought. "No, that's a prince." She laughed again, her face alight with amusement. "And I'm not even a princess, so I guess I'm safe."

"What wizard?" Dave asked blankly, as he turned her firmly in the direction of the staircase that led to the upper level of the ranch-style house.

"Is there more than one?" she asked, turning toward the corner of the room where Damon was still holding court. She knew exactly where he was, even though she'd been careful not to glance at him after that first searing exchange. She had been as aware of him as if they'd been linked by a golden cord. Perhaps they had, she thought hazily, but the cord was invisible. Sorcerers could weave spells like that, couldn't they? She realized she had been a little afraid of him, but the emotion was gone now. She wasn't afraid of anything at the moment. "Joel Damon, magician extraordinaire!" She lifted her glass in a mocking salute.

He was gazing at her as she knew he would be. She'd felt his eyes on her all evening and it had engendered a tiny flame of excitement she had refused to acknowledge. He wanted her. Desire for her was there, blazing openly and hungrily in his expression, but there was something else as well. An anger and resentment so intense it pierced even her present buoyant self-confidence. "Perhaps you're right; maybe I shouldn't press my luck." She smiled impishly up at Dave. "He might not realize I'm not a princess."

"At the moment he's looking at you as if you're a full course dinner after a month-long fast," he said, his lips tight. "I think I'd better get you out of here before he decides to gobble you up." He was propelling her rapidly across the room toward the stairs. "Home," he said firmly.

"If you say so," she agreed cheerfully. "However, I don't know why you think there's anything wrong with me."

"Who is she?" Joel's voice was clipped. His gaze followed Balding and the chiffon-clad woman as they slowly climbed the stairs. Balding's arm was clasped around her waist with a casual intimacy that scraped like rough sandpaper on Joel's nerves. Not that it was any more caressing than the fondling they had been indulging in all evening, he thought darkly. They couldn't seem to keep their hands off each other and were obviously seeking privacy for greater intimacy. He pulled his gaze away from them with no little effort and turned to scowl at the slim dapper man next to him. He'd been resisting asking about the woman all evening and wasn't the least bit pleased that the impulse had finally overcome his strength of will. "And what the hell is she to Balding? Didn't you tell me he was married?"

Ron Willet, his assistant director, raised a mocking brow as he watched the couple who were now entering a bedroom on the second level. "He's very much married—and to an extremely nice lady from what I hear. But marriage wouldn't stop many men when a sexy little siren like that one makes herself available to them." His eyes narrowed as they moved to Joel's face. He had been aware all evening that Joel's attention had been caught by the chestnut-haired beauty and had been surprised that his boss hadn't made a move on her. In the five years he'd worked with Joel, he'd never known him to hesitate when it came to taking what he wanted, particularly when it was a woman. And if he read the signs right, Ron knew that Joel wanted this one very much. He had noticed a smoldering intensity about Joel this evening that had aroused his curiosity. "She's some eager little starlet, I imagine. It's your party; don't you know who your guests are?"

Joel shook his head, his frown deepening. "My secretary appears to have issued invitations to half the film colony. I usually leave it up to her." His lips twisted. "It doesn't really matter. The faces may change, but the personalities stay essentially the same."

"I saw that luscious little blonde hanging on to you earlier in the evening." Willet's eyes twinkled. "She looked vaguely familiar. Have you used her before?"

"In one of my pictures or in my bed?" Joel

asked rhetorically. "Neither, thank you, but she has aspirations for both positions. She's the second woman tonight who's made sure I knew that she'd be 'passionately' grateful if I decided to cast her in that minor role in *Venture*." He took a hefty swallow of his brandy. "For God's sake, the part is barely a walk-on and half the women in Hollywood are willing to throw themselves on the traditional couch and spread their legs for me. I wish to hell casting would get busy and give the role to someone, and get these women off my back."

"*I* should have your problems," Willet said dryly. Then he suddenly chuckled. "Though perhaps they're beginning to filter down to us lesser mortals. Balding is obviously reaping the benefit right now with that lovely upstairs. She probably thought he'd be an easier nut to crack than you." He shook his head admiringly. "What a fantastic body. Do you think I could persuade her to believe I have more influence with you than Balding does?"

Joel felt a totally unreasonable rage surge through him. "You think she's wheeling and dealing?" he asked tersely. Why did the idea annoy him so much? It was exactly what he'd decided she'd been doing all evening.

Willet shrugged. "Seems logical. Most of the women in town who are as gorgeous as she is are fledgling actresses, and I wouldn't say Balding is the type to sweep a woman off her feet. She certainly was more than a little affectionate with him. Add it up for yourself."

"I already have," Joel growled. His brooding gaze returned to the closed bedroom door. "You're right. The picture couldn't be much clearer." He had known as well as Willet what the woman was up to, but for some reason he hadn't wanted to admit it. And that was as unreasonable as all his other reactions to the sexy little hooker had been!

He'd heard of instant explosive attraction, but he had never really believed it existed until tonight. Now he could hardly deny what was an obvious, physical fact. Very physical, he thought wryly.

He liked to be in complete control of all facets of his life and this sudden compulsive magnetism filled him with a nameless uneasiness. My God, he'd been as jealous as hell when he'd seen Balding put his hands on her, yet he hadn't so much as exchanged one word with her. He didn't even know her name, dammit. This was utterly insane. When he had seen her start up those stairs with Balding, he had felt a possessive rage that was totally alien to him . . . and utterly new.

Willet had been watching the expressions chase across Joel's face. "I gather you'd like a chance at Balding's little starlet yourself," he commented. "Why don't you deal yourself into the game? You hold more aces than Balding could ever hope to draw. I'm sure the lady wouldn't be adverse to changing partners if you cared to show her it would be worth her while."

"Your faith in my fatal charm is hardly flattering," Joel said caustically. "But in this case your assumption is probably correct. I've had too much experience with the *genus* starlet and I'm well aware of their priorities."

He had no doubt he had the necessary muscle if he cared to exert it. Besides, a chemistry as dynamic as what he had experienced couldn't be one-sided . . . despite the cool little game she had been playing throughout the evening to pique his interest. And that last little mocking toast she'd thrown him before she'd gone upstairs with Balding had been redolent with challenge. But he wasn't at all sure it was a challenge he wanted to meet considering the volatility of the emotion she seemed to be able to provoke in him. He had an idea it would be much safer for him to stay away from the source of that turbulence.

"You're not interested?" Willet asked. "You're going to leave her to Balding then?"

"No!" The violence of his reply surprised even himself. He drew a deep breath and made a conscious effort to regain his usual composure. His fierce response to the idea of Balding making love to her had caught him off guard. But at least it had answered the question he had been asking himself.

A reckless little smile curved his lips as he finished his brandy in one swallow. Why the hell had he hesitated anyway? He had always had a taste for the bizarre and unusual and this response certainly qualified in that area. There was no way he was going to let another man take what he oddly felt was his own. He thrust his empty glass at Willet. "Get rid of this, will you, Ron?" he asked. "I think perhaps I'll follow your advice and sit in on the game. It might prove interesting." He turned and strode across the crowded room to the staircase.

Dave opened several doors, finally discovering the guest bedroom that was obviously being used as a cloak room. There was a closet open, jammed with furs and velvet cloaks of every description, and the king-size bed was overflowing with other wraps. "Oh, there's nothing wrong with you; you couldn't be more right," he said caustically. "You always worry about wizards turning you into frogs." He shut the door behind them. "What does your wrap look like?"

"It's chiffon and it matches my gown," she said absently. "I wasn't worrying about him turning me into a frog. I told you they only bewitch royalty."

"It's not here." He turned from the closet,

moved swiftly over to the bed, and began to toss wraps carelessly aside as he searched for the scrap of cinnamon chiffon. "It's probably on the bottom; Sheila's always is."

"I'll find it." She joined him at the bed and knelt on the area he had cleared with his ruthless pillaging. She quickly located the sheer bit of chiffon and waved it triumphantly. "Got it." She draped the stole dramatically over her chestnut head and around her lower face like an Oriental veil. "Come with me to the Casbah," she intoned huskily, her brown eyes dancing.

"Dammit, quit kidding around," Dave said in exasperation. His hands closed on her shoulders as he prepared to haul her off the bed.

"I can see how you might be annoyed."

The voice was deep and faintly cynical. Kendra didn't have to glance at the figure leaning indolently against the door jamb to know it was Joel Damon. She wasn't even surprised.

"When a lady invites you to accompany her to a bedroom, it's very frustrating when she starts playing games instead of getting down to the business at hand." Damon strolled into the room and closed the door with utmost care behind him. His smile deepened and seemed oddly feral to Kendra. "And I trust it *was* business, pretty lady?"

Dave released her and straightened slowly. "I think you have the wrong idea, Joel," he said quietly. "I was just about to take her home. We were looking for her wrap."

"Of course you were," Damon said smoothly as he strolled over to the bed and stood looking down at Kendra. She was conscious of a curious tension beneath that mocking control and saw a flicker of that bewildering anger in the depths of his eyes. His hand reached out to push the chiffon veiling from her head and it fell to her shoulders. "I'm sure you were having an exceptionally good time doing it, too. I really should apologize for barging in, but I was compelled to interrupt you. There are some reporters downstairs and we wouldn't want to give them cause to write about the orgies at my innocent little get-together, now would we?"

Orgy? Dave and her in an orgy? It was too much! Kendra threw back her head and laughed.

Damon cocked his head; his eyes narrowed on her face. "You have the sexiest laugh I've ever heard," he observed bemusedly. "I heard you laugh several times tonight, but I was too far away to hear you speak. Talk to me, pretty lady."

Her eyes locked with his in an intense, mesmerizing stare. Then she smiled impishly. "My name is Kendra Michaels. And I'm *not* a princess."

"How unfortunate," Damon drawled. "But I'm sure you have many other attributes. That hoarse throaty little voice is definitely one of them. It reminds me of the sound a kitten makes when it runs its claws over velvet."

"I think she's had a bit too much to drink, Joel." Dave's voice was wary. "I'd better take her home."

That was the second time Dave had accused her of that. "I'm perfectly sober," she said indignantly. "I told you I've only had two glasses of champagne."

"You heard the lady." Damon's lips twisted cynically. "She knows exactly what she's doing. I rather thought she did."

"Of course I do," Kendra said firmly. Ahh, but if she had thought him a sorcerer across the room downstairs, it was a mild witchery compared to his spell at close range. His olive eyes were even more brilliant and mesmerized her with a force as potent as the most magic elixir. She licked her lower lip nervously and his gaze followed the motion with a heated absorption that made her breath leave her body. "But maybe Dave's right and I'd better go home."

"Yes, we'd better leave." Damon's voice was a little thick. He turned abruptly to Dave and said crisply, "I'll take care of her. Go on downstairs and play host for me. God knows I'm bored enough with the role."

"You'll take her home?" Dave frowned uncertainly.

"Do you think I'm going to ravish her on the spot?" Damon asked evasively. "I told you I didn't want any orgies at my party. It's very bad form. We'll leave in a few minutes. I just want to get to know Miss Michaels a little better."

"Kendra?" Dave asked.

Poor Dave, she thought. He was obviously concerned about her and it was equally evident he didn't want to offend Joel Damon, who could make or break his career with the utmost ease.

"I'll be fine, Dave," she said gently. "Mr. Damon can take me home. Why don't you do as he says?"

"If you're sure." There was an unquestionably relieved expression on Dave's face as he turned toward the door. "I'll give you a call in the morning, Kendra."

The door had scarcely closed when Damon dropped down on the bed beside her, pushing her from her kneeling position back on her heels. His hands were gentle on her bare shoulders but nevertheless she was startled. Then his hands were gone and she felt cold and lonely.

"It was wise of you to let him go," he murmured. "I think if you had offered any objection at all, Dave actually would have put up a fight. That says quite a bit for the potency of your sex appeal, because Dave's a very ambitious young man."

"I know," she murmured. He was sitting so close she could feel the waves of heat emanating from him while the scent of clean soap and a cologne that had a fresh spicy fragrance assaulted her nostrils. "He knows exactly where he's going. I admire that about him."

"Like-to-like?" he asked, his tone caustic. "I can see how an ambitious little lovely like you would feel a certain fellowship with Balding." His eyes narrowed. "Did you know he's married?"

Her eyes widened. "Of course! What difference does that make?"

He laughed mirthlessly. "None evidently. Not to you and certainly not to Balding after the vamping you did tonight. I don't have to ask if you got what you wanted from him."

"What I wanted from him?"

"The job," he said impatiently. "Did he promise everything you wanted on a silver platter or was he waiting for you to deliver first?"

She stared up at him in bewilderment. "Yes, he gave me the job. I've already signed the contract."

Joel's lips tightened grimly. "Well, I'm afraid you'll just have to renegotiate—especially the clause concerning fringe benefits. All those will be awarded to me from now on." His expression softened as his hand smoothed her hair with featherlike strokes. "You won't be disappointed. I wield a hell of a lot more power than Balding and I always keep my word."

Fringe benefits? He wasn't making sense, but it didn't seem to matter as long as he continued to stroke her hair with that gossamer touch. How long had it been since she had felt so wondrously pampered? "Sorcerers always wield an enormous amount of power," she said dreamily. She turned her head to rub her face on the hand stroking her hair. He really had lovely hands, strong and tan, with long graceful fingers that spoke of sensitivity and creativity. Beautiful hands that burned the soft smoothness of her cheek. "Your touch makes me feel so strange."

Strange wasn't the word for it, he thought wryly. He'd never even conceived of an emotion this powerful. Why the hell did she have such an effect on him, he wondered irritably. It wasn't as if Kendra Michaels was the most beautiful woman he'd ever met. Her figure was a little too curvaceous for current tastes, and her wide-set brown eyes were too large for the thinness of her face. Her lips were lovely, but they looked more vulnerable than sensual. Yet when she had run her little pink tongue over that full lower lip, he had felt a jolt of pure desire that had caused his loins to swell and his heart to pound crazily. It must be her gorgeous coloring that was so provocative. She was all rich, golden sheen from the clear olive skin to the auburn-burnished chestnut hair rippling down her back in gentle silken waves. An impatient scowl darkened his face as he remembered the insane burst of possessiveness that had exploded inside him when he had first caught sight of her. Mine, he'd thought with instant certainty. She's going to be mine.

"Is it strange for you, too?" Kendra asked.

"Oh yes," he muttered. "It's like that with me too." His hand wandered down to encircle her throat, his thumb pressing gently in the soft hollow. "I hadn't the slightest doubt that it would be from the moment I first saw you."

She was gazing up at him with the grave wonder of a child. "You're angry, aren't you?" she whispered. "I can feel it in you. Why are you so angry?"

"I'm not angry," he denied quickly, knowing that he wasn't telling the truth. There was a slow burning resentment deep inside him that was aimed more at himself than at her. The longer he was with her the more conscious he became of that loss of cool control. He shrugged. "Perhaps my emotions are a little confused at the moment. I can't say that I like my reaction to any woman to be quite this violent." His eyes narrowed on her face. "You *are* aware that this thing between us couldn't possibly be termed *ordinary.*"

"Yes," she answered absently, her gaze still on the well-defined curve of his lips. Those strange mesmerizing eyes had caused her to overlook how sensitive and beautifully shaped they were. "You have a lovely mouth; do you know that?" Her index finger reached up to trace the sensual line of his lower lip. It felt smooth and warm beneath the pad of her fingertip, and she knew again that breathless little tingle. His lips parted suddenly to capture her finger and for the briefest instant she felt the sharp nip of his teeth before he released it.

"The better to eat you with," he said lightly. She could see that the pulse in the hollow of his throat was throbbing jerkily and there was a slight flush in the hollow of his cheeks. He slowly leaned forward until their lips were only a breath apart. "And eat you up is exactly what I intend to do, sweetheart. You're a feast that would tempt the gods and I find I'm a very hungry man." Each word was a tiny warm puff of breath that was a kiss in itself. "Hungrier than I've ever been before. I want to devour every bit of you."

Hungry he might be, but when his lips finally closed on hers they were gentle, almost tentative. They brushed and moved against hers like a connoisseur who wanted to savor the delicacy of the bouquet before he permitted himself to taste the wine itself. And the giving and taking was intoxicating enough to Kendra that her breath caught in her throat.

"Delicious." Joel's voice was tremulous and his heavy lids half closed to veil the smoldering glint in his olive eyes. His hands tightened on her shoulders and he brought her closer with utmost care so that her chiffon-covered breasts were resting lightly against him. "But I think we both need a little more solid sustenance, don't you, Kendra?" This time when his lips touched hers they were still gentle but firmer and the demand greater as the kiss progressed to a sweet sultry languor. "Give me your tongue, love," he muttered, parting her lips to flowering fullness. "I want to taste you. I want to know the textures of you."

She wanted to know that about him too, she thought dreamily. Suddenly it seemed the most vitally important thing in the world to learn everything she could about the exciting physical presence of Joel Damon. She gave him what he'd asked for and heard him utter a deep groan that sounded for all the world like the contented growl of a domesticated animal.

His lips closed on her tongue, using a gentle suction to draw it from her. Once her tongue was lured deep into his mouth, he began a leisurely exploration that caused her to press closer against him. With a little moan, she opened her lips wider. His tongue was searching, probing, touching, moving over the roughness of her tongue. She could tell that everything he found was wildly pleasing to him by the mad pounding of his heart against her own and the gasps of hunger and delight that broke from him when he paused for breath. The pauses were ever so brief before he plunged once more into the sensual pool of pleasure that was their joined mouths.

To have such an effect on him, to know that

she could cause the sorcerer to tremble and groan with the same fiery magic that he was weaving in her gave Kendra a wild, primitive satisfaction. Her heady sense of power only served to increase the exhilaration she was experiencing. She broke away with a little breathless laugh, her face alight with delight. "It's wonderful!" Her hands curved around his neck to thread through the hair at his nape. "It's like flying; it's like skydiving; it's like . . ."

Her lips covered his with an eagerness that made his muscles harden against her softness. It was he who finally broke the hot, fluid contact. He lifted his head and drew in a deep breath as if his lungs were starved for oxygen.

"Well, no one could accuse you of being coy," Joel said. His lips twisted wryly as he looked down into her eyes, sparkling like rich cognac. "Are you always this frank and straightforward?"

Her hands were running caressingly through his thick, dark hair. It felt as clean and vibrant as the rest of him. "I try to be," she said vaguely. Her face clouded as she remembered that she hadn't been entirely honest tonight with either Dave or Skip. How could she have been when there was so much at stake? But she wouldn't think of that now. It brought a return of the crushing heaviness that seemed to be always with her and that, miraculously, had lifted for the last few hours. "Sometimes it's not so easy," she said uncertainly. "But I like to think that I'm a fairly honest person." Her face was as troubled as an open, innocent child. "Does it matter to you?"

He felt a sudden melting tenderness that was as poignant as it was unexpected. She looked so vulnerable and unhappy after her brief burst of joyous merriment that he felt a surge of fierce protectiveness, completely at odds with the desire wracking him. Immediately he experienced defensive anger. Dammit, what was the woman doing to him?

"Your honesty matters a hell of a lot," he said at last and with soft menace. "You won't find me very lenient if you ever decide that being honest with me is a little too 'difficult' for you, Kendra. I won't tolerate you cheating on me. While we're together, there won't be any other men in your bed." His lips curved in a mirthless smile as he gazed down at her bewildered face. His hand deliberately fell from her shoulders to the curve of her buttocks and brought her swiftly into the cradle of his hips so that she could feel the bold hardness of his arousal. His smile deepened at the gasp that she gave as her hands clenched spasmodically on his shoulders. "As you can see, I plan to keep you very occupied from now on."

Then without waiting for her to reply, his mouth was once again on hers and this time there was no tentativeness and very little tenderness. His hot passion was so intense it was almost brutal. She made a soft moan of protest that was almost inaudible. He must have heard it, however, for abruptly the harshness ceased though the tenderness didn't return. Instead, he practiced a skilled voluptuousness that wooed her into blind, submissive need. She writhed in his cupping hands like a wild thing. Her lips and tongue responded to him with a thirst that mirrored the hunger she felt in his tense, hard body.

He broke away and there was a look of grim satisfaction on his face as he took in the wild rose flush on her cheeks and the bruised softness of her lips. "You're a very hot lady, Kendra Michaels," he drawled, a flicker of triumph in his eyes. "Which is damn fortunate for me. If I'm going to be caught in this sweet little trap, I'll be damned if you won't be there with me."

"Trap?"

"Never mind." He was suddenly on his feet and lifting her from the bed. "Come on, let's get out of here." He picked up the chiffon wrap from where it had fallen on the bed and drew it carefully around her. Then he was grasping her by the wrist and pulling her toward the door.

"But where are we going?" she asked, startled. She was knocked totally off balance first by the most intense, sensual euphoria she'd ever experienced and now by this sudden about-face.

"If we stay here another five minutes, all those coats and capes are going to end up on the floor and we're going to be between the sheets." His lips tightened grimly. "And everyone downstairs will put two and two together and be trying to imagine just exactly what we're doing to one another in that bed." He shot her a dark glance. "Ordinarily, I wouldn't give a damn, but for some reason I'm feeling as possessive as the devil about you. I won't let those bastards run their thoughts over you any more than I will let their hands." He paused at the door to take out his pristine white handkerchief and dab at her lips. "You're a little mussed," he said and smiled as his other hand tidied her hair. "Delightful, but too obvious all the same."

He opened the door and propelled her down the corridor, his hand cupping her elbow with an impersonal courtesy.

"We're going back to the party?" she asked, confused. They started down the stairs.

"No way," he said, adroitly avoiding a couple standing on the bottom step. He gently guided her across the foyer to the front door. "We're getting out of this zoo."

She tried to push the shock and disappointment away. She didn't want to go home. She had never known such magic. She wanted it to go on and on forever. "You're taking me home?"

"In a manner of speaking," he answered quietly, an enigmatic expression on his face. He opened the front door and allowed her to precede him. "Yes, we're going home now, Kendra."

Two

"*Illusion de l'Arc en Ciel.*" The headlights picked out the beautifully scripted engraving on the stone gatepost and Kendra repeated the words softly. "*The Illusion of the Rainbow.* What a strange name for a house."

Joel raised an eyebrow quizzically as he pressed the button on the dashboard that electronically opened the iron gates. He had been silent since they left the house in Laurel Canyon. She hadn't minded his quiet moodiness once she realized he had no intention of driving her to her apartment in Fullerton, but to some unknown destination of his own. She hadn't been curious about that destination either. Content, she let her head loll on the plush silver gray headrest, while her eyes feasted on the sight outside the passenger window: the star-strewn, glittering blanket of the sky. Occasionally her gaze had roved to the dark, intent face of the man at the wheel.

"*Illusion de l'Arc en Ciel,*" Joel said. "So you know French."

"Only a little," she said as she watched him drive through the gates that slid silently closed behind them. "High school stuff. Why *The Illusion of the Rainbow?*"

He laughed with genuine amusement. "Do you know that's the first question you've asked me since we left the house? You're placing a remarkable amount of trust in a complete stranger. How do you know I'm not whisking you away to some isolated retreat for some S and M games?"

How ridiculous he was. Sorcerers didn't have to resort to whips and bondage when they could have anything they wanted by exerting their potent magic. "I just do," she said serenely. "Why *The Illusion of the Rainbow?*" she persisted.

He shrugged. "Why not? There's nothing real about a rainbow. It's a mirage, a dream: here for an instant and vanishing the next. All of life is like that if you think about it. Nothing is really stable enough to hold on to for more than a moment." His lips curved in a curiously bittersweet smile. "So when I create something, anything that may become special to me, I build in a safety device to remind me of the evanescence of the rainbow. It saves me from foolish emotional involvement."

What an incredible degree of weariness and vulnerability was contained in those few terse words. They pierced the clear golden bubble that surrounded her and the poignancy of feeling caused her throat to tighten achingly.

"And is this house special to you?" she asked gently. "I never heard about any other house of yours except the one in Laurel Canyon."

"You might say it's special," he said with a wariness that sent a surge of maternal tenderness through her. "I needed a place to come to when I couldn't stand all the phoniness anymore. I had the estate transported almost stone for stone from its site in France—Normandy to be precise—and then had it renovated to my specifications." He shot a mocking glance at her. "It has a dungeon, but no torture chamber, I assure you." His expression changed to total seriousness. "And no one knows about this house for the very good reason that I paid a small fortune in hush money to keep it that way. Even my secretary doesn't know about *Illusion de l'Arc en Ciel*. I'd have reporters and sycophants crawling all over the place if there were a leak." His voice deepened with intensity. "And this place is *mine*, dammit."

The Mercedes abruptly swung around a curve in the road and Kendra caught her breath in surprise at the sight that met her eyes.

He'd called it an estate but it resembled more an old Norman Keep complete with drawbridge. Its ancient stone walls shone dull silver in the moonlight, and it was set among a thick grove of trees like a small elegant castle from another age should be. No, not elegant, she thought. The Keep was too primitive to be termed elegant. It was no fairy-tale palace but a fortress of tranquility. A warrior's last bastion of defense.

"It's very . . . impressive," she managed to say at last. It was more than that, she thought as they crossed the lowered drawbridge and passed into a little cobblestone courtyard. It was as revealing as a spotlight on the man behind that mocking sorcerer's mask, and suddenly she wanted to know more, understand more about him than his physical magic that had so captivated her. "How long have you owned it?"

He got out of the car and came around to open the passenger door. "I first saw the Keep when I was a boy of seven. My mother and I were staying at a château a few kilometers away and I would run away and spend the entire day on the grounds whenever I got the chance." He helped her out of the car. Slipping an arm around her waist, he propelled her toward an enormous oak door in a shadowy recess. "I suppose a real fortress had a certain fascination for a wild young hellion straight from the hothouse atmosphere of the proper château his mother dominated. I felt somehow that the Keep belonged to me. I took one look at it and I knew it was mine." He opened the door with a key that was ridiculously tiny given the apparent size of the lock. One of Joel's renovations, she thought hazily as he pushed open the door and fumbled at the wall. His voice echoed hollowly in the darkness. "It's become something of an obsession with me. When I was a boy in school, I'd hoard my allowance until I had enough to buy the furnishings and little art objects that occasionally came on the market from the Keep."

The enormous hall was suddenly illuminated by electric candles in the huge central chandelier. "About seven years ago, the Keep itself came on the market and I bought it and had it shipped over here and reassembled."

"You waited a long time," she murmured, her gaze going around the room with wondering eyes.

She could understand why Joel's voice had echoed. The ceiling of the hall must have been fifty feet high and timbered in rich oak, as was the wide staircase that led to the balcony surrounding the second floor. The walls and floor were composed of the original smooth block stone and had a stark, brutal beauty that was softened by the richness of the cream and burgundy area rugs on the floor. A magnificent medieval tapestry graced the wall over a mammoth walk-in fireplace. The fireplace was large enough to roast an ox and probably had been used for just that in the distant past. She was jarred out of her appraisal by Joel's hand on her elbow urging her toward the staircase.

"There have been very few things in my life I've found worth waiting for, but when I do find one, you'll discover I have a great deal of patience." He was propelling her up the stairs. "However, you'll notice I'm very short on that quality at the moment, so it's fortunate that it's not necessary in this case." His lips curved mockingly. "It simplifies things enormously that we understand each other so well, doesn't it, Kendra?"

Understand each other? He may have felt that he understood her, but in spite of her occasional flashes of clarity about his personality she was still very much puzzled by him. Somehow that fillip of uncertainty only added to the excitement and exhilaration she was experiencing as she allowed him to lead her up the stairs and then through another door on the upper level. It led to a steep circular stone staircase lit by electric torches affixed to the curved walls. The tower, she thought vaguely, enjoying the sound of their footsteps on the smooth stone. It was all like a lovely dream—coming to this ancient stronghold and moving with Joel through these echoing corridors toward a mysterious secret chamber at the top of the world. Would there be steaming cauldrons and balls of crystal in the warlock's lair? At the moment she felt anything was possible—even probable—and the prospect filled her with even greater anticipation.

That anticipation was more than fulfilled when he unlocked the chamber at the top of the stairs and stepped aside so that she could precede him into the room. She had expected magic and magic she received—if not exactly the kind associated with crystal balls and potent elixirs.

So flooded with light was the stark aesthetic chamber that she first thought the room was artificially illuminated. Then she realized it was moonlight that was cascading through the glass-paneled walls and etching chessboard patterns of light and shadow in the conically shaped room. Kendra moved slowly into the room and gazed around her incredulously. It was like being in the center of a greenhouse or a crystal-faceted genie bottle. The leaded glass walls started only a few feet from the slate floor and towered to a point some thirty feet above her. The only furnishings in the room were a king-size bed that was covered with a simple white wool spread and a chest at the foot of the bed with polished brass bracketing.

"This room is magnificent," she exclaimed softly. "I've never even imagined a place like this could exist." She turned toward Joel who was watching her from a spot near the door. "I can see why you said it was special to you." Her eyes met his across the room and she knew a strange melting sensation as she rushed on hurriedly, "Thank-you for sharing it with me." Then, as he still didn't answer but continued to gaze at her with an unnerving intentness, she faltered. "But I'm afraid I don't understand why you did. Share this lovely place, I mean. You've really never brought anyone here before?"

"I haven't the slightest idea what possessed me to bring you here." He closed the door and leaned against it indolently. "I've been known to give in to errant impulses on occasion. Perhaps it was that." He shrugged. "Or maybe it was because I had the exact same sensation when I first caught sight of you as I did when I first saw the Keep. A rainbow lady for my place of rainbows. Perhaps I just wanted to see the two of you together." His hand went to a mother-of-pearl switch on the wall.

"Stand still, sweetheart, and indulge my whim. I'll turn on the exterior lights."

Place of rainbows. Suddenly the bedroom became just that as the intricately placed lights came into radiant play and she realized what caused that chessboard effect. The panels weren't all clear glass as she had originally supposed, but interspersed with delicately tinted shades of shell-pink, spring-green, azure, topaz, and rich violet. Rainbow colors were pouring into the room like the brilliant rays of an alien sun. It turned the pearl-gray slate of the stone floors, as well as the simple white wool spread on the king-size bed, into a sea of color, and she realized why the room was furnished with such severe restraint. Any embellishment would have been totally unnecessary in the center of a rainbow.

"Ahhh. . . ." Joel expelled his breath in a soft burst of satisfaction. His gaze fixed on her as she looked up at him in startled wonder. She was bathed in a ray of pure golden light that turned her skin to tawny amber and her chestnut hair to bright flame. "Yes, that's why I brought you here. That's what I wanted to see. You're a very lovely illusion, Kendra Michaels." He was moving very slowly toward her. "It's really a pity that you're not real." He was so close she could feel the heat of his body as he halted before her; he was also caught in the prism of golden light. His lips twisted cynically and he looked like a gilded statue of Lucifer.

"But I've grown accustomed to illusions, so why should it matter? Particularly when this particular one is so willing to accommodate my every whim?" His head bent and his lips lightly brushed her naked shoulder causing her to inhale sharply at the little tingle of shock that shook her.

She couldn't breathe for a moment, trying to steady the pounding of her heart as she felt the warmth of his tongue moving across her throat, then the gentle nip of his teeth at her earlobe. She could smell the lovely aroma of him again as she had in the bedroom at Laurel Canyon. Her senses were assaulted by a deluge of sensations. Could anything be more beautiful than standing here in the center of this exquisite rainbow mist and letting Joel touch her in this thrilling way? She'd never realized that lovemaking could be so magical. She had always thought she must be a little cold, that her rough and tumble upbringing had instilled in her the tomboyishness that precluded the explosive sexuality she was feeling now.

But she had never had a sorcerer like Joel Damon to perform this magic, she thought dizzily, as his hands fell on her bare shoulders and then curved around her nape to tilt her head back and give his lips the freedom to explore the arched column of her throat. That probably made all the difference.

"Beautifully willing, beautifully responsive. What more could a man want?" His lips moved to the sensitive flesh beneath her chin. "And you are that willing, aren't you, rainbow lady?"

"Yes, I'm willing," she finally said aloud. His satisfied chuckle jarred her. There was a note of triumph in the sound that disturbed the joyous serenity filling her. Her behavior with Joel tonight was completely out of sync with the way she usually behaved, but it hadn't seemed to matter. Nothing had seemed to matter except grasping this lovely moment before it slipped away and she was plunged back into the tension and worry of everyday life. Yet hadn't Joel Damon made several enigmatic and bitter comments this evening? And now she could feel that tension and smoldering resentment even as he touched and caressed her. There was something wrong, something that should be said. Something that she should understand.

"Joel, I think we—"

"Don't think." His hands were threading through her hair and his voice was suddenly harsh. "Rainbow ladies shouldn't think. They should only feel." His lips were on hers and his tongue invaded her mouth, receiving its moist sweetness. His hands tugged gently at her hair as his lips left hers. "And touch. Touch me, Kendra. I want to have your hands on me."

She felt that now familiar breathlessness, accompanied by the sensation of melting. "I want that, too," she said faintly. Her palms came up to rest lightly against his chest; her fingers brushed the lapels of his jacket aside. She could feel the abrupt jerk of his heart beneath her hand and the heat of his skin through the fine material of his dress shirt. Then she was eagerly unbuttoning his shirt and slipping her hands inside to run them curiously over the hard muscular wall of his chest. She closed her eyes, savoring the delicious smoothness of his sleek warm flesh covering that exciting hardness of tendon and muscle. She could feel her palms tingle as the blood rushed to the sensitive surface. She took her time exploring the thatch of dark wiry hair on his chest and the tiny male nipples that hardened with amazing speed. Her fingertips brushed lightly over their rigid nubs. She heard him chuckle and her eyes flew open.

"I thought I could stand a little erotic foreplay, but I hadn't counted on my responses being quite so urgent." He took a step backward and drew a deep, shaky breath, releasing her. "I think it's time we indulged another of my fantasies. Let me see how you look gowned in rainbows, love." He shrugged out of his jacket and tossed it carelessly on the low chest at the foot of the bed. "I want to undress you myself."

His hands reached out to cup the fullness of her breasts through the chiffon, and her breasts instantly responded. His grasp tightened around her, his gaze fastened on the pale cleavage bared by the gown. "God, I can't wait to see you," he said thickly. "I want to lose myself between your breasts. I want to use my tongue and teeth on them and see them come alive for me." His thumbs brushed the engorged tips of her breasts and said teasingly, "I'm glad to see that you feel the same way, sweetheart." He drew her close, his hands searching for the fastening of her gown. His lips brushed her temple in a butterfly caress as he slowly eased the zipper down her back. "You feel so good against me," he whispered, his tongue stroking the inner curve of her ear.

A shiver ran through her that had nothing to do with the temperature. Kendra felt as if she were burning up, the blood racing through her veins at a pace that was almost painful. She sagged against him, her knees as shaky as the time she had made her first parachute jump. When his hand slipped inside her dress to rub the naked hollow at the small of her back, she flinched as if touched by a hot brand. A little moan broke from her and her hands wound around his waist as she clung to him almost desperately. "Joel, it's crazy," she said. "I never—"

"Do you think I don't know that," he interrupted roughly. "None of it makes sense." His deft hands were feverishly molding and stroking the smooth satin of her back. "I've barely touched you and I'm so ready I'm aching like hell."

She heard the trace of resentment mixed with desire in his voice, but this time she didn't even try to interpret it. She was too lost in sensation to be conscious of anything but the aching emptiness that throbbed deep within her.

Then Joel was pushing her gown down over her hips until it fell to her ankles in a pool of diaphanous chiffon.

She heard Joel's breath catch and then expel sharply as his eyes regarded her with lingering possessiveness. She stood before him wearing only a minute pair of satin bikinis and her high-heeled sandals, but she felt no embarrassment or shyness. She thought of her body as a useful tool and cared for it with the same impersonal attention. She had a good body, strong and graceful and in most cases capable of meeting the demands she put upon it. Now Joel was about to demand something entirely different, and she was responding with an eagerness that left no room for hesitation.

He slowly reached out a hand to hover over one full breast. He shook his head in dazed disbelief. "Good Lord, I'm trembling!"

So was she. She could scarcely breathe, her lungs so constricted that they allowed only the most shallow of breaths. Suddenly overcome with an urgency and impatience that brooked no more delays, she leaned forward so that her nipple nestled into his palm. "Touch me *now*." Her voice was a low, throaty murmur. "Please, I can't wait any longer."

"Neither can I." His hand closed around her with a desperation that was almost painful. "Oh God, neither can I." He lifted her breast, his head bent, his face taut with hunger. "I need you. I need all of you." His lips were on her nipple, his tongue stroking her with warmth, with fire, with impassioned need.

Joe raised his head, his face heavy with sensual languor. "I told you I wanted to devour you," he said huskily. "I think we'd better move to the bed before I lose control completely." His arm encircling her waist, he half led, half carried her across the room. Even as they walked he refused to relinquish tactile contact. His hips brushed hers with every step, while his hand on her breast moved caressingly over the velvet pink aureole. "I don't want to let you go even for a minute. Lord, I'm hungry for you, Kendra."

Then they were beside the bed, on the bed, his weight crushing her into the mattress. He was on top of her, his arms extended on either side of her bearing his weight as he looked down at her. The misty light was a delicate pink on the white coverlet, bathing her smooth skin in its soft light and turning the tips of her breasts a deep, rich carmine. "Beautiful," he muttered, lowering himself to rub his hair-roughened chest against her softness. "All beauty and color and . . ." His face suddenly contorted with pain and his muscles tensed. "Damn, I knew I wouldn't be able to wait. I want you too much." Rolling off her, he stood up, tearing off his clothes with desperate speed, his eyes never leaving her face. "Look at me," he urged softly, as he tossed the clothes aside. "I want you to see how much I want you, what you do to me." He lay down beside her, mesmerizing her with his eyes. "I want to watch your face while I do all the things to you I've been thinking about since the minute I first saw you."

His lips covered hers with a slow, heated sensuality, his tongue entering to taste and tempt her own. When he drew back, his eyes were glazed and smoky with desire as they searched her flushed face. "That's what I want to see. *Want* me, rainbow lady, for heaven knows I want you!"

Want him? Oh yes, she wanted him. The roughness of the hair on his chest against her sensitive breasts made her feel like she was being stroked with fire. Now his hands brought her into the hollow of his hips so that the physical evidence of his need was pressed against her, with only the scrap of satin separating them. He was rubbing against her like a giant cat, his eyes narrowed on her face to catch every expression, every nuance of desire. As he watched, her head began to thrash back and forth on the pillow, her breath coming in little whispering gasps.

Then he was still, his breathing labored. "Sweet rainbow lady, are you ready for me to love you now?"

"Oh yes." Her hands clutched at his shoulders as he removed the last barrier of material between them.

"I'm glad you agree." He parted her thighs and slipped between them. "I'm not sure I could have waited if you hadn't." The heel of his hand rested on the soft, curly down that protected her womanhood, making it his own, stroking and petting her lovingly. It was both arousing and incredibly tender, and it made her feel deliciously treasured. He leaned forward, his hand still caressing her, and covered her lips with a kiss of infinite sweetness. Then, with a wild, bold passion, he thrust forward with a strength and force that shocked her. There was a white-hot, tearing pain, and then she was full of him and her cry changed to a guttural cry of satisfaction.

He froze into statuelike immobility and she heard him utter a shocked exclamation against her lips. He tried to raise his head, but her arms tightened around his neck and she buried her hands in his hair. Her lips reached for his as her legs curled around his hips to draw him deeper into that breathless unity. His hips moved in a rhythm that had an element of desperation in its forcefulness.

The explosive intensity of the pace at first stunned her senses, leaving her to cling to him in an agony of wanting. Then she was aware of a different need. She wanted to give as well as take the ecstasy Joel aroused with every thrust. She began to move, arching up to him in a rhythm of her own, watching his face intently to see the pleasure she gave him.

She wasn't disappointed. He lifted his head with a low groan that was half growl, and his expression was infinitely sensual. Kendra felt a jolt of pure, primitive satisfaction.

"You're driving me insane." His words were punctuated by the swirls of sensation that spun through the rainbow mists surrounding them. "That's right, love, move. Come to me."

How could she help coming to him, she thought hazily. He was absorbing her, piercing her, not only with his body but with his sorcerer eyes and his words of need and desire. She could see the delicate rainbow rays of pink and gold and violet beyond the naked bronze of his shoulders, and it only deepened the beautiful, physical reality of their lovemaking. He had to be wrong, Kendra thought. This was no illusion, no ephemeral *arc en ciel*. Its brilliance was increasing with every passing second, every move, every breath. Then, with a shimmering burst of color that was like the birth of a world, she found it. She felt Joel tense above her and heard his low, savage cry as his arms tightened possessively around her. He sensed it too, she thought joyfully. It belonged to both of them.

He was quiet in her arms, his body heavy upon her, and she could feel the beat of his heart against her breast. Then he rolled over, his arms still clasping her to him. One hand stroked her hair lazily as his lips brushed the delicate veins at her temple. She curled up contentedly against him, her head nestling into his shoulder like a trusting child. She was suddenly so weary she could hardly keep her eyes open, but the sorcerer had given her his gift of joy and she felt compelled to say something.

"Thank you." Her voice was a drowsy murmur, as she cuddled closer. "Thank you very much, Joel."

His chuckle reverberated beneath her ear. "You're very welcome, rainbow lady," he said. "Thank *you*. I think we can consider this a very even exchange of pleasure." Just then his relaxed body stiffened warily against her. "Or was that what you meant? Perhaps you were talking about the part? You should have held out for a bigger role, sweetheart. In a town like this, there aren't that many women who have what you had to trade. Virginity has a definite appeal for a certain type of man. I for one find it very exciting to know I was the first. You would have been wise to capitalize on that." The hand stroking her hair suddenly tightened spasmodically. "But don't worry, sweetheart, you won't lose because of your inexperience in negotiating this agreement. I'm always ready to pay a fair price for what pleases me. I'll make sure that the next role is juicy enough to satisfy even the most ambitious tastes." His tone became mocking. "However, you'll have to promise to stay in my bed and continue to please me. Agreed?"

She didn't answer and his voice hardened to steel. "I wouldn't try to bargain too hard if I were you, Kendra. You'll find I can be very determined and I don't hesitate to be as ruthless as I need to be to get what I want." He tilted up her chin; his eyes narrowed on her face. "You'll give me exactly what I . . ."

His voice trailed off as he noticed that her russet lashes were closed and her breathing deep and even. How much had she heard before she drifted off so peacefully? Probably not much, judging by how soundly she was sleeping. His lips curved in wry amusement as he realized that she had once more wrested control of the situation away from him—and without even trying.

Why wasn't he feeling the resentment he'd known earlier, instead of this weird protective tenderness? His throat felt oddly tight as he noticed how vulnerable she looked with her lips parted slightly in slumber. He pulled the white wool coverlet over them and then carefully, gently, he brought her closer into his embrace.

Mine.

Even before Kendra opened her eyes she was conscious of the familiar little ache in her lower back and the even sharper one behind her eyes. She sighed unhappily, and nestled closer to Joel's comforting warmth. Joel?

Her lids flew open and her gaze focused in shock on the mat of coarse black hair on Joel Damon's chest. Oh Lord, what on earth had she done? Then, as the memories and sensations of last night tumbled helter-skelter back to her, she realized very well what she had done. Rainbow mists and a sorcerer's green eyes and a driving, explosive physical magic. How many times had he taken her last night?

She bit her lip in vexation. How stupid to worry about how many times they had made love when the obvious problem was that it had happened at all! How could she have done such a thing? Ending an evening in a stranger's bed might not have been all that unusual for some women, but it was for her, dammit. It was even more bizarre for her to abandon herself to a hedonist like Joel Damon, who was also her boss. For someone who prided herself on her professionalism, there couldn't be a bigger mistake. Had it been the painkiller she had taken that was responsible for this insanity? She had rejected that idea last night, but she was beginning to wonder now. Perhaps in combination with the champagne she'd drunk . . . oh, she just didn't know. Maybe it was the man himself who'd caused this temporary insanity. He had certainly had an incredible impact on her senses even before her abrupt mood change. Well, the catalyst didn't matter now. The only important thing was that she had regained her usual cool sanity and could act accordingly.

She scooted carefully away from Joel Damon. With any luck she could get out of here without waking him and avoid a confrontation that would be excruciatingly awkward.

Luck wasn't with her and she was still struggling with the zipper of her gown when Damon's eyes flicked open. He was instantly wide awake. "Going somewhere?" he asked as he sat up and regarded her intently. "Your bed manners leave a little to be desired, sweetheart. Haven't you ever heard that a good mistress makes herself available in the morning as well as at night? Take off your gown and come back to bed, Kendra."

Kendra could feel the color rush to her cheeks as she hurriedly yanked at the zipper. "I'm afraid that won't be possible, Mr. Damon," she said as her eyes searched the floor wildly for her shoes. "I have to leave now. As soon as I finish dressing, I'll be on my way."

"Mr. Damon?" he echoed blankly. "Isn't it a little late for that degree of formality? If I remember correctly, a few hours ago those long, lovely legs were wrapped around me and I was—"

"That was a mistake," she interrupted, her

cheeks definitely scarlet now. "I wish you'd just forget last night ever happened." She spied one sandal half under the bed and pounced on it. "I realize the entire situation was as much my fault as it was yours, but it still should never have happened." Where was the other damn shoe? "I'm sure when you think about it, you'll agree that working together would be very difficult if we allowed any personal relationship to interfere." How had that shoe gotten under the covers of the bed? "I promise to stay out of your way as much as possible when I come to Sedikhan."

He muttered a low curse, his face darkening stormily. "Trying to back out of our agreement so soon, Kendra? I believe I warned you about that last night. I'm not settling for a one-night stand when I had a more permanent arrangement in mind." His green eyes were glacier cool. "You'll get the part and all the additional roles I can manage to throw your way, but I'm the one who calls the shots. Now get out of those clothes and come back here."

"The hell I will." Her brown eyes were blazing as she stomped into her sandals. "On the set you may call the shots but that's the only place, Mr. Damon. I haven't the slightest idea what you're talking about, but I'll be damned if I'll stand here and let you threaten me like some kind of petty dictator. Last night was the only time I'll ever be in your bed and it would be wise if you'd recognize that fact. As soon as I finish this job, I'll take pains to avoid working on any more of your films." She tossed her head angrily. "I'm going to have enough on my plate just handling the gags on this picture without having to tolerate a director with a colossal ego."

"Gags?" His eyes narrowed.

"Gags," she repeated impatiently. "Stunts.

You're a director, you know what I mean, for heaven's sake!"

"Yes, I know what you mean," he said, his expression grim. "I think you'd better come back here and sit down. We've got some talking to do. So you're not an actress?"

"An actress?" Her eyes widened in surprise. "Of course not. What ever made you think that? I've been hired to do Billie Callahan's stunts in *Venture.*" Then all the pieces of the puzzle fell into place and she glared accusingly at him. "You thought I was sleeping with you to get a part in *Venture*?"

"Sleeping had very little to do with it," he drawled, "but yes, I thought that's why you were vamping Balding, then me." His lips tightened. "Upon reflection, it could still be reasonable. The business you're in is very competitive and *Venture* has a big budget."

"Sell myself into your film? I'm a professional stuntwoman, not a hooker," she spat. "I'm very good at my job and I have no need to earn any fringe benefits on my back." She drew a deep steadying breath and tried to control her temper. "As for Dave, I've been friends with him and his wife for years. He'd laugh himself silly at the idea that I was trying to vamp him."

"You could have fooled me," he said, scowling at her. "You two were all over each other last night."

"Affection, not lust," she said caustically. "I suppose it would be too much to expect you to recognize the difference. You were so busy dreaming up dirty little pictures with that fertile imagination of yours. You wanted me to be some kind of prostitute so that you could feel comfortable about going on the prowl yourself. Not that you need any excuse from what I hear."

"No, I don't." He leaned back on the pillows and regarded her calmly. "And I believe I could be excused for the mistake under the circumstances. You weren't exactly reluctant to be lured into bed, Kendra, and you displayed a very satisfactory degree of lust yourself." He paused. "For an amateur."

She inhaled sharply, feeling as if she had been hit in the stomach. "I told you last night was a mistake. Perhaps Dave was right and I had too much to drink." Her gaze was steady. "I won't be dishonest and try to shift the blame onto your shoulders." She tried to smile. "Suppose we both chalk it up to temporary insanity and just go on from here."

"I'm willing," he said promptly. "Come back to bed and we'll initiate a brand-new start for our relationship."

"Haven't you been listening to me?" Her hands clenched in exasperation. "It's not going to happen again. It shouldn't have happened at all. I don't want one-night stands either, and I certainly have no intention of becoming your mistress even temporarily. I don't have the time or the inclination to play the games you specialize in, Mr. Damon."

"Joel, dammit," he grated out. "And you had plenty of inclination last night. Give me five mintues in this bed and I'll guarantee you'll develop an inclination." His voice softened to a velvet murmur. "Remember how it was, rainbow lady? Remember how you loved my hands on you." His green eyes were glowing softly. "In you. How you went crazy when I made you wait for it? But I didn't make you wait long, did I, Kendra? I couldn't, I had to—"

"No!" She was remembering all too clearly and his words were bringing pictures to mind that she had successfully submerged since she'd awakened in his arms a short time ago. It was all coming back with a vengeance now. Damon's sleek muscular body bathed in soft delicate hues bending over her, his face dark and heavy with passion, his hands cupping . . . No! She wouldn't think about it. It was over and done with.

But the rainbow rays were still bathing the room. Sometime during the night Joel must have gotten up and turned off the exterior lights, for it was sunlight that was pouring into the room now. In its way, it was even more beautiful, she thought dreamily, and Joel was beautiful too. His hair was rumpled. His eyes were shining jewel-bright in that cynical face. She could feel a stirring in her breasts as she recalled those eyes glazed with need looking down at her and shook her head in desperate rejection.

"No," she repeated. "I don't remember. I won't remember. I'm no rainbow lady, no matter what you call me. I have substance and I'm one of the most pragmatic people you could ever hope to encounter. I have no more need for your whimsical little illusions than for the role you want to cast me in." She wearily brushed her hair from her face. "I'm sure you'd grow bored with me very quickly, but I'm afraid I can't indulge you even for the short time it would take. My life isn't any illusion; it's very real and very earnest." She turned to leave. "Now if you'll excuse me, I'd like to go. Don't bother to get up; I'll phone for a taxi."

"I have no intention of excusing you," he said quietly. "And you'll have a difficult time making that call. I've never had a telephone installed here." When she whirled to stare at him in surprise, he shrugged casually. "I told you I wanted to be removed entirely from my usual lifestyle. A telephone would be the first leak in the dam." His lips curved in an ironic smile. "So, since you're more or less marooned here until I see my way clear to driving you home, why don't you make yourself comfortable?" Then as she opened her lips to speak he held up his hand. "Fully clothed if you insist." His lips quirked. "That's a giant concession, you understand." He patted the bed briskly. "Sit down, we still have some talking to do."

Kendra cautiously approached the bed. "I think we've exhausted the only subject we have any mutual interest in." She halted a few feet away.

"We haven't even started," he said coolly. "It's obvious I'll have to reopen negotiations, as you aren't an actress after parts in my films. I have to fly to Sedikhan this evening to set up the production and I want you on that plane with me. What can I offer to insure that you'll come with me in a capacity that we'll both enjoy? I can promise you I'll be willing to give you anything within reason." He shrugged. "Perhaps anything beyond reason. Try me."

She shook her head in disbelief. The man was stubborn as the devil. "Listen carefully," she said, speaking very distinctly. "I refuse. No sale. I'm not interested. *Nyet.* Is that clear? I'll be arriving in Sedikhan in a month as provided in the terms of my contract and not before. And when I do arrive, it will be to perform the job I was hired to do." She turned and marched toward the door. "I think that about covers it." The door closed behind her with a decided click.

Joel smiled in amusement and grudging admiration as he threw off the covers and got out of bed. It was clear Kendra Michaels was indeed going to be something of a challenge, but one he was confident he could handle. He took his time dressing and strolled leisurely downstairs. He had the keys to the car and Kendra couldn't get very far on foot in those flimsy high-heeled sandals. He'd pick her up in the Mercedes before she reached the gates. Then they'd continue their discussion to *his* satisfaction.

His complacency was shattered to smithereens when he opened the front door. The low purr of the Mercedes was the first sound he heard and then Kendra's mischievous little laugh as she reversed the car and drove past him through the courtyard.

Her eyes were dancing as she saw his dumbfounded expression. "I hot-wired it," she called out the window. "I told you I was a very pragmatic person, *Mr.* Damon."

With a mocking wave, she drove out of the courtyard and over the rumbling wooden drawbridge.

Three

Kendra was just entering the customs line after deplaning in Marasef when she became aware of a slim, jean-clad figure calling her name and waving wildly at her from beyond the barricade.

"Kendra Michaels?" the girl shouted cheerfully above the noisy bustle of the airport. "I'm Billie Callahan. I just thought I'd let you know that I was here to meet you. Arriving in a foreign country can be kind of intimidating. You'll be through here in just a few minutes and I'll drive you to the location. Okay?"

"Okay." Kendra smiled back gratefully. She had been on Mideastern locations before and she doubted if the actress would prove correct. She'd probably be stuck here for an hour, but it was nice of the woman to take the time to come to meet her.

To her amazement her processing through customs was both polite and superefficient and she was walking through the barricade to join Billie Callahan within the predicted few minutes.

"You were right," Kendra said blankly as she piled her luggage in the baggage tote and fastened it securely. "I think that's the fastest I've ever cleared customs in any country. It's quite a surprise."

"Sedikhan is a surprise in most ways," Billie assured her. "I've been here five weeks and I still keep discovering new, exciting things. You'll find all goverment functions glide on greased wheels here, thank heavens. Sedikhan is an absolute monarchy and the ruling head is Alex Ben Rashid, who evidently runs a very tight ship."

"You've been here five weeks?" Kendra asked, puzzled. "I thought they only started filming three weeks ago."

"They did." Billie gave a brisk order in Arabic to the waiting porter and he immediately grasped the tote and took off at a trot through the crowded airport. "I talked Joel into sending me out early. I like visiting new places." She grabbed Kendra's arm. "Come on, the jeep's parked in the short-term lot and our porter is tearing through the airport like that football hero in the car rental commercial."

"You speak Arabic?" Kendra asked as she obediently fell into step. "After only five weeks?"

Billie made a face. "Not very well. It's a sinfully difficult language to learn. I lived with an Arab couple for the first three weeks and picked up quite a bit. I can generally make myself understood." She looked Kendra over with frank interest. "Lord, you're gorgeous." She sighed. "And what fantastic bazooms. I look more like a boy than a girl. No sex appeal whatever. Sometimes I wonder what Joel was thinking about when he hired me."

Kendra burst out laughing. There was something terribly appealing about Billie Callahan and she could see very well why Joel had hired her. Skip was right, however. Kendra would definitely have to bind her breasts to double for the ingenue. They were both of medium height, but Billie was slimmer and her delicate bone structure gave her a porcelain fragility.

That delicacy was completely belied by the crackling vitality that emanated from her. Her faded jeans and strappy sandals were mated with a loose thigh-length tunic, striped in vivid pink and burgundy that should have been a horror with the wild mop of copper curls that tumbled past her shoulders. Instead, it only served to complement that gypsylike vivacity. But it was Billie's unusual face that probably had fascinated Joel Damon. Though not conventionally lovely, it possessed a quality that was poignantly stirring to the senses. The curve of her lips was tender and compassionate and she had the misty violet eyes of a dreamer.

"Beauty isn't all that important for stardom anymore," Kendra said soothingly. "Being a good actress is much more essential."

Billie groaned with mock glumness. "I wish you hadn't said that. I'm a lousy actress. After this picture I'll probably never do another one. I just hope I can muddle through *Venture* without disappointing Joel."

"You don't seem too upset about the possibility of such a short and mercurial career," Kendra said curiously. "I gather being a movie star isn't one of your top priorities?"

Billie shrugged. "It's interesting enough for a while, but I'll probably be ready to move on by the time the picture is finished. I usually get too restless to stay in one place for long."

They had reached the jeep and Billie was helping the porter stow the baggage in the back with strength surprising for one of her apparent delicacy. In a few minutes she had tipped the porter and was negotiating her way out of the parking lot into the crowded street.

She darted Kendra a curious glance from enormous eyes as dark as wood violets. "Now if I had a job like yours, I might have more staying power. It must be a real kick to take the chances you do and get paid for it. How did you get started in a business like stunting?"

"I grew up in it," Kendra answered. "My father was in the business all his life and when other kids were tumbling down sliding boards and playing on the teeter-totter, my brother and I were learning how to fall off thirty-foot towers into swimming pools without breaking our necks." A nostalgic smile curved her lips. "It's a good thing we were too young to have sense when we first started or we'd have been scared to death. As it was, by the time we realized just how dangerous some of the stuff we were doing was, it was old hat."

"Didn't your mother object to all those shenanigans?"

"Why should she? She was in the business herself before she married my father. Then after Casey and I were born, they decided it would be more responsible if one of them quit stunting." Her smile was sad. "They didn't want to take a chance on leaving us orphans. It's rather ironic that it happened anyway. A drunk smashed into their car on the freeway and killed them both."

"Is your brother a stuntmen, too?"

"Not anymore," Kendra murmured. "He's studying to be a lawyer now." She'd been gazing with interest at the passing scene and remarked, "I had no idea Sedikhan would be so modern." Tall skyscrapers, wide, busy streets, and late model cars all reflected a strong economy. Even the dress was principally Western and up to the minute.

"The citizens of Sedikhan have one of the

highest per capita incomes in the world. They have so much oil here that it staggers the imagination," Billie said. "I heard they have an entire government department just to think up ways of spending their income." At Kendra's snort of disbelief, she grinned impishly. "Well, it's almost true. Ben Rashid has been trying to yank his country out of the last century and into the space age. You'll see what I mean in a minute. But get off the main thoroughfare and you're back in the land of flying carpets and veiled dancing girls."

"And we're going to be getting off the main thoroughfare?"

Billie nodded as she turned into a side street. "Joel's leased practically an entire village outside of Marasef for the location, but it takes forever if we keep to the main drag. One of the extras told me about a short cut that should get us there in a jiffy." She cast Kendra a mischievous glance. "Even if it doesn't, there's no harm done. You'll get a chance to see a little of the Arabian Nights of Marasef." Her voice lowered dramatically. "You'll find it sinfully fascinating, dahling."

Sinfully. Apparently that was one of Billie's favorite adjectives, Kendra thought in amusement, yet there was nothing in the least wicked about her *joie de vivre*. And the side streets they traveled were fascinating. The streets were narrower here and they they had to stop twice to avoid hitting a pushcart with a gaily striped awning and then a donkey loaded with copper pots and pans. There were no skyscrapers here, but only flat-topped houses with arched windows, one on top of the other. The clothing of the pedestrians was different also. The men wore flowing burnooses for the most part and the few women she spotted were garbed in dark, shapeless draperies.

"Well, at least the women aren't wearing veils,"

she commented. "Feminism has made a few strides here."

"That's because all you're seeing on the street is the more liberated segment of female society," Billie said dryly. "The men in Sedikhan still have very firm ideas about the place of women in the general scheme of things."

"Joel Damon must feel right at home here," Kendra said absently and then could have bitten her tongue at the curious glance Billie shot her. She had thought she had successfully blocked out all trace of Joel Damon for the past month, blast it.

"You know each other well?" Billie asked, turning off into a deserted byway. "He did mean to meet your plane, you know. Then he got tied up with—oh my God!" She stomped on the brake with a force that almost threw Kendra through the windshield. "They're going to kill him!" Billie jumped out of the jeep and started running down the street.

Kendra stared bewilderedly after her and then straightened in shock as she saw Billie's objective. A huge wild-haired Arab was pinned to the wall of a building by two burly toughs in flowing robes. His face was bruised and cut and even as she watched, a fourth man with a Vandyke beard ran a wickedly curved knife down the victim's cheek leaving a trail of blood. She was out of the jeep in a flash dashing after Billie.

Billie gave a loud piercing shriek that resembled a coyote in agony. It brought all three of the men whirling toward her with startled faces; the one wielding the knife let loose an angry cry.

"Billie, no!" Kendra shouted. But Billie wasn't listening as she dove toward the bearded man like a tornado and fastened desperately onto the arm wielding the knife. She uttered that nerve-jarring shriek again and butted her head violently against the bearded man's nose.

Kendra expected to see that deadly knife plunged into Billie's stomach. Oh Lord, why on earth had Billie done this?

But help came from an unexpected source. Evidently the two men who had been holding the bleeding man captive had loosened their grips at Billie's surprise attack, because the giant suddenly exploded into action. He jerked free. His left arm backhanded to slam one of his former captors against the wall; his other hand darted out to deliver a numbing karate chop that knocked the knife from the bearded man's hand.

Kendra reached them and retrieved the knife, then grabbed a struggling Billie, pulling her away from her still dangerous antagonist. "Billie, dammit, you're going to get yourself killed! We can't fight these men alone. We'll have to go for help."

But it appeared that no help was needed. Now that he was free, the bushy-haired victim seemed to be more than competent to handle the situation. He was holding the bearded man by the throat with a grip that was turning the man's face a livid hue, while his elbow slammed into the man on his right. With an incredible swiftness for one so large, he whirled and lifted his knee in an agonizing blow to the loins of the man on his left, then with crushing force bashed together the heads of the other man and the bearded knife wielder. It was over so quickly that Kendra could only gasp as she watched the three men sink to the ground in various states of semiconsciousness.

Their bruised and bloody Samson wasn't waiting to enjoy his victory, however. He turned and took both women by the elbows and ran down the street half pushing, half carrying them along.

Behind them they heard a dazed groan and a shout of rage just as they reached the jeep. They scrambled into the vehicle and Billie reversed, then made a screeching U-turn that almost threw Kendra out of the passenger seat and caused the fierce Arab in the rear to cling grimly to the seat in front of him.

Then they were racing recklessly down the cobbled street. Kendra cast a frantic glance behind them to see one of their pursuers stop in the middle of the street, lift a furious fist, and shout what was obviously an obscenity at them. Billie turned the corner and they were once more back on a busy thoroughfare. Kendra sat back with a sigh of relief as Billie eased up on the accelerator.

"I think we lost them," Billie said breathlessly. "Damn, I was scared."

"You could have fooled me," Kendra said dryly. "Do you often take on three murderous brutes like those or did you simply want to provide me with a little local color?" Suddenly she began to laugh. "I have to admit you're right, Billie. I certainly found our little side excursion *sinfully* fascinating." She glanced at the scowling barbarian in the backseat. "And just what do you intend to do with him?"

Billie was frowning uncertainly. "I don't quite know. I guess we'll wait until we get to the outskirts of the city and let him out. I wouldn't want those men to catch him again."

"Not after you almost got yourself drawn and quartered rescuing him." Kendra chuckled, then shook her head wonderingly. "And you thought being a stuntwoman would liven up your life. At least I get paid for taking chances."

"Well, there really wasn't anything else I could do," Billie argued defensively. "I couldn't let a helpless man be hurt, perhaps even murdered, could I?"

"He didn't look exactly helpless when he was wiping the streets with those three thugs." Kendra raised a brow in skepticism. "For a while I was even feeling a bit sorry for them. *I* certainly wouldn't want to run up against our friend in a dark alley. He looks like a cross between Mr. T. and Bigfoot." Her gaze ran over the Arab's white shirt and baggy dark trousers tucked into soft beige suede boots. "With maybe a little Bedouin bandit thrown in."

"I think it's all that wild shaggy hair," Billie said, gazing into the rearview mirror. "I'm sure he could be very civilized looking in Western clothes." She shrugged. "Well, it's not really important. Everything turned out for the best. Neither one of us was hurt and we managed to rescue Hercules here. We'll just drop him off and continue on our merry way."

When they pulled over to the side of the road a few minutes later, it appeared that Billie was woefully incorrect. Judging by the heated exchange in Arabic between their passenger and Billie and the growing frustration on her face, it was proving a far from satisfactory confrontation.

"What's going on?" Kendra asked in a temporary lull in the battle.

Billie ran her hand distractedly through her mop of coppery curls. "His name is Yusef Ibraheim and I think he wants to adopt me or something," she said in exasperation. "As much as I can make out with my fractured Arabic, he feels a certain responsibility for me since he's sure I saved his life. Oh Lord, I thought it was only the Chinese who had ideas like that."

Kendra tried to keep a straight face. "He can't be over thirty, so I think adopting you is out. Perhaps you misunderstood his intentions."

"Well, I think I got the gist of it," Billie said gloomily. "It seems Yusef here has an overdevel-

oped protective instinct. That's why he was being
worked over by those hoods today. He was working
as a bouncer in a bordello in town and he objected
very strongly to the way one of their influential cus-
tomers was abusing one of the girls." She made a
face. "He objected so strongly in fact that he broke
the man's arm. Evidently the man hired some local
gangsters to exact a bloody revenge."

"Charming," Kendra said, her lips twitching.
"Just like a 1930s screenplay. May I ask what you
intend to do with our gigantic friend?"

Billie sighed as she started the ignition. "I
guess I'll have to take him back to the location with
us. It will be safer to keep Yusef out of town for a
few weeks and maybe by that time I'll be able to
convince him I can take care of myself." She bit her
lip. "I don't know what Joel will say. He's probably
going to murder me. He's going to be mad as the
devil anyway after I took off with the jeep to come
and get you."

"You weren't supposed to pick me up at the
airport?" Kendra asked, her eyes widening in surprise.

Billie shook her head. "I took off on my own
when I heard Joel was tied up. Ron, the assistant
director, was supposed to make the trip, but I persuaded him to let me come instead." She grinned
impishly. "After all, Dave Balding arranged for us
to share a cottage together. It was only natural that
I'd want to meet my roommate, right? It was completely irrational of Joel to think I might get into
trouble just driving to the airport."

"Oh yes, totally unreasonable." Kendra
couldn't hold the laughter in any longer. She could
almost sympathize with Joel Damon trying to control a puckish elf like Billie. "Nothing could possibly happen to you just picking me up."

"Well, that's what I thought." Billie sighed.

"Why do these things always happen to me? I'm really a very responsible person."

"I'm sure you are," Kendra said gently. Billie might be a bit eccentric, but her actions today had been anything but irresponsible. On the contrary, her passionate conviction that she was her brother's keeper had almost gotten her killed. And now she was prepared to shoulder the additional burden of that ferocious albatross in the backseat. She might be faulted for a bit too much generosity of spirit and too impulsive a nature, but not for irresponsibility. "Don't worry; we'll work out some way to keep your Yusef safe and still out of your hair."

What was she letting herself in for? Kendra wondered ruefully. As if she weren't going to have enough trouble trying to persuade Skip to give her that special, while attempting to keep her relationship with Joel strictly professional! Now she found herself involved with this appealing pixie and her possibly criminal guardian angel.

"Did I hurt your back when I made that turn?" Billie asked, frowning in concern.

Kendra quickly jerked her hand away from her back. Drat, she'd have to watch that. "No, of course not." She smiled reassuringly. "I had a little accident a few months ago and I still have a twinge or two on occasion."

"That's good," Billie said, relieved. "I could just see me lugging in your limp and broken body, as well as Yusef, here." She grimaced. "Joel would probably strangle me. You know how protective he is of his friends."

"No, I don't know that," Kendra said, her tone reserved. "We're not really friends, merely acquaintances."

"Really? Then why was he so angry when he couldn't pick you up himself? He's too busy a man to provide taxi service for all and sundry. He didn't even pick up Brenna Donovan when she arrived three weeks ago, and she's the star of the picture."

"Skip told me she had the lead," Kendra said quickly, hoping to distract her. "How is she to work with?"

"Super." Billie's face lit up. "A certified doll. You'll find everyone on the picture a joy to work with." She wrinkled her nose distastefully. "With the exception of the male lead, Dirk Danford. He thinks he's God's gift to womankind."

"Problems?"

"Not for me. I'm not sexy enough to rate a pass from the great lover, but he's giving Brenna a rough time."

Kendra whistled. "He likes to live dangerously, doesn't he? I've heard Michael Donovan is absolutely crazy about his wife and possessive as all get out. Having a producer like Donovan put you on the blacklist is professional suicide."

"Dirk thinks he's safe," Billie said, her lips tightening grimly. "Donovan's tied up in London with postproduction on *Siren Song* and Brenna's too much of a pro to complain to Joel. She thinks she should be able to handle it herself."

"And you don't think she can?"

"Perhaps." Billie's violet eyes were narrowed and thoughtful. "But gentle people like Brenna sometimes have trouble fighting off pests like Danford. She just may need a little help."

Oh Lord, another rescue? Kendra groaned inwardly. She had an idea that being the roommate of Billie Callahan might be more dangerous than jumping that jeep across the canyon.

Four

The stucco house in front of which Billie pulled up looked identical to all the others on the hard-packed dirt street. It was small, white-washed, and had the flat roof and arched windows she had noticed in most of the other houses around Marasef. The door was painted bright scarlet, and leaning against it was a dusty and perspiring Dave Balding. He straightened slowly, his warm smile of welcome swiftly fading as he caught sight of the bruised and bleeding giant in the backseat.

He hugged Kendra absentmindedly when she got out of the jeep and turned to Billie with a scowl. "I was wondering what took you so long. Joel was about to send a search party to try to locate you. We might have known you'd find some trouble to keep you interested."

"That's not fair," Billie said indignantly. "I couldn't help—"

"I know, I know," Dave interrupted with a

resigned sigh. "You never can, Billie. But I haven't got time to listen to the story right now. Joel stationed me here to wait for Kendra and bring her over to his trailer the minute she showed up."

Kendra tensed and then forced herself to relax. She had known she'd have to face him sometime. Why should she feel this sudden sense of panic?

"But I have to see Joel right away," Billie protested. "I have to explain about Yusef and get Joel to find him a place to stay."

"You're keeping him?" Dave asked, gazing at the Arab warily. "He looks a little dangerous for a house pet." He shrugged. "But so was the baby lion you bought in the bazaar last week. Joel probably won't let you keep this one either."

"This is different. I can't let Yusef go back to Marasef," Billie said, worriedly gnawing at her lip.

"She's right, Dave," Kendra said. "Billie's discussion with Joel is much more important than anything he'd want to say to me. He's probably just being polite and wants to welcome a new member of the team to Marasef." She was relieved she had an excuse to postpone that first interview with Joel. "I'll just wash off the travel grime, change clothes, and report to him later. Where is his trailer located?"

"Two streets over," Dave answered, "on the edge of the village. Everyone except Billie is quartered in house trailers. She opted for inconvenience and atmosphere instead." He was frowning uncertainly. "And I don't think you're right in believing Joel will give Billie's wild man a higher priority than you. He's just likely to tear a strip off me for not obeying his instructions."

"Nonsense," Kendra said briskly. "Help me take my bags inside and then you can go with Billie and Yusef to get their problem solved. It's a much more sensible plan." She reached for the large suitcase beside Yusef and suddenly found the Arab beside her, a bag under each massive arm and one in each hand. He nodded commandingly toward the door and Kendra found herself obediently opening it and stepping aside for him to enter.

He strode briskly through the central living area and through the beaded curtains that served as a door to the room at the rear of the house. He plopped the suitcases down beside one of two beds that was more a narrow couch with a multitude of colorful cushions scattered upon it. He turned to look at her impassively, his bulk appearing even more intimidating in the small room.

"Thank you," she said faintly, her eyes wide in surprise. He seemed to understand though. His dark face remained expressionless as he nodded curtly, brushed by her, and strode back through the house out the front door where Dave and Billie hovered.

Kendra followed in his wake. "I can see what you mean by him being overprotective," she told Billie dryly. "I don't think I've ever had such a forceful bellhop."

Billie was beaming at her charge like a proud mother. "I told you everything would work out. Yusef will adjust to the situation in no time at all. Come on, Dave, let's take him to see Joel."

But would the rest of the film company adjust to Yusef, Kendra wondered in amusement as she watched the jeep disappear around the corner at the end of the street. She was still smiling as she walked back into the house and closed the door.

Her smile slowly faded as she once more crossed the large room and pushed aside the curtain of amber beads to enter the sleeping area. She could feel the familiar cold lassitude flooding every muscle now that she had let down her guard. More than anything she wanted to lie down on one of those scrumptious-looking couches and sleep for a week. Surely it wouldn't hurt to rest for just fifteen minutes? She gazed wistfully at the couch's inviting spread. Then, reluctantly shook her head, picked up one of the suitcases, and placed it on the bed. She knew better by now than to pamper herself with a nap. Her bone-weariness had been growing steadily of late; that fifteen minutes probably would stretch to the entire evening if she fell asleep as she had done a lot recently.

Panic raced through her, but she quickly suppressed it. There was nothing wrong with her that a week's rest couldn't put right. She assured herself staunchly that the only reason she was feeling so exhausted was because of the grueling experience of finishing that picture Bodine directed. Skip was right. Bodine was an incompetent ass of a stunt coordinator. As soon as she finished *Venture* and had the most monstrous bills paid, she'd be able to take a month or so off and relax. But not now. She mustn't give in now.

She opened the suitcases and pulled out fresh underthings, a pair of khaki slacks, and a loose tunic top in a dull army green. When she entered the bathroom, she discovered what Dave had meant by Billie opting for atmosphere rather than convenience. The little alcove adjoining the bedroom contained only a toilet, basin, and a chipped, clawfooted bathtub that must have been fifty years old. Would it be too much to hope for hot water, she wondered morosely. She made a face as the cold brownish water poured from the curved nozzle. On second thought she would take a sponge bath and explore the possibility of a hot shower later. There had to be someone who had decent bath facilities on this location.

She had completed her bath, slipped on the khakis and tunic and was putting her hair up in a high ponytail when she heard the front door open and then close with a decisive slam.

"Kendra!"

The voice was rough and angry and undeniably that of Joel Damon. She sighed resignedly. So much for her plan of confronting him in the businesslike atmosphere of his office. She called, "I'll be out in a minute." Perhaps she could keep him out of the bedroom.

She should have realized how futile that hope was. When she came out of the bathroom, it was to see him pushing impatiently through the beaded curtains, a dark scowl on his face.

She tried to ignore the sudden jump of her pulse at the sight of him. It wasn't joy; it was a mere chemical reaction to an attractive male, she assured herself quickly. Dressed in dark jeans that hugged the strong line of his thighs and a cream sweatshirt that complemented his darkness, he looked virile enough to excite any woman.

"Hello, Joel," she said coolly. "You needn't have taken the trouble to come and see me. I told Dave I'd report to you as soon as I changed. I realize how busy you are."

"Report?" Joel asked caustically. "You sound like a private talking to his CO. Dave gave me your message and you'll be happy to know that it annoyed me just as much as you intended it to. Why the devil didn't you come as soon as you arrived, blast it?"

"You *are* my CO in a manner of speaking," Kendra said quietly. "And Billie's business was more important than my strictly perfunctory courtesy call." She lifted an inquiring brow. "Where is she, by the way?"

"At the first aid tent repairing the damage to her newest acquisition."

"You're going to let Yusef stay?"

"I don't have much choice unless I want Billie moving into town to protect him," he said with exasperation. "At least I can keep an eye on both of them here." He drew a deep breath. "And now that we've disposed of the subject of Billie and her wild man, will you kindly tell me where you've been for the last month? I've been calling your apartment every evening since the day I arrived in Sedikhan and there's been no answer. I even checked the listing personnel gave me with the phone company to make sure it was a working number."

"You tried to call me?" Kendra asked, her eyes widening in surprise.

"I just said so, didn't I? You knew damn well I wouldn't let you get the last word after you took off in my car and left me to walk five miles to the nearest town to phone for a taxi."

"That far?" A tiny smile was tugging at Kendra's lips. "What a pity."

"I can see your heart's bleeding for me," Joel said dryly. "I could cheerfully have murdered you by the time I got back to the house in Laurel Canyon and found the Mercedes, but no Kendra Michaels."

"You deserved it," she said serenely. "You're a very arrogant man and like to get your own way entirely too much, Joel Damon."

"You liked my way very much too that night a month ago," he said softly. His expression suddenly became grave. "Where have you been for the past month, Kendra?"

"I had a job to finish before I started *Venture*. I was on location in Colorado." She had trouble now in meeting the intensity of his green eyes. "We had said all we had to say, and there wasn't any need for you to phone me anyway. I'm sorry if your ego was stung a little."

"Hell yes, I was stung . . . and annoyed," Joel

said crisply. "But that wasn't why I was trying to get in touch with you. After I got over the first anger, I started to worry, dammit."

Her forehead knitted in puzzlement. "Worry? What about?"

"What do you think?" he asked, scowling. "I didn't protect you. I thought you'd be on the pill. How was I to know that you were the last virgin left in Hollywood?" He ran his hand through his hair. "I was afraid I might have made you pregnant."

"I see." She felt as stunned as if she had been struck by lightning. She had never even considered the possibility that Joel had broached. She had been so busy trying to block the man out of her thoughts that the possible repercussions of that night had also been repressed. And those repercussions were a very real possibility, she realized numbly. No, she was panicking for no reason. Just because she was a little late was no need to worry. She was often irregular, particularly when she was under the sort of stress she'd been under the past few months. She smiled with an effort. "I can see how you might have been a little concerned. Poor Joel, did you think I was going to try to involve you in a paternity suit? Or were you going to give me a nice fat check and the name of an exclusive little abortion clinic in Beverly Hills?"

"Shut up!" Joel's voice was oddly husky. "Is it too much to believe that I was genuinely worried about you? That I didn't want you to suffer for the pleasure you gave me, that we gave each other? I wanted to let you know you could count on me if it proved necessary." His green eyes were searching. "Is it necessary, Kendra?"

"How very gallant of you," she said, not looking at him. Why was she feeling this aching pain because of the notion that it was only obligation prompting Joel's concern? "I'd never heard you had such a keen sense of responsibility, Joel. It's very old-fashioned to—"

She broke off as he crossed the room in three swift strides. His hands grasped her shoulders and gave her a little shake. "Give me a straight answer, dammit. Are you pregnant?"

She glared up at him defiantly, her eyes suspiciously bright. "Of course I'm not pregnant," she said, her throat tight and painful. "So you needn't worry that I'll come to you with any demands on either your conscience or your bank account."

She could see the relief wash over his face and it brought a fresh jab of agony that was totally unreasonable.

"You're sure?"

"Very sure," she lied with a shaky little laugh. "I'm sorry to insult your virility, but it *was* only one night."

"Thank God," he breathed fervently. "Lord, I was worried, sweetheart." His arms slipped around her with the utmost naturalness and cradled her to him with a simple affection he had never had the chance to show her before. "I kept thinking of you all alone and having to contend with a problem like that." His lips gently brushed her temple. "It nearly drove me crazy. It won't happen again, I promise. I'll make sure of that. I'll take care of you from now on." His hands were running up and down her back in a caress that was both soothing and exploratory. "You're thinner than the last time I held you. You feel almost breakable in my arms. Didn't you eat at all when you were in Colorado?"

She leaned against him like a weary child. There was no threat, no demand in the arms that held her. There was only tenderness and caring and a lovely protectiveness that made her feel marvelously treasured. "Sometimes," she said, nest-

ling her head under his chin. "Most of the time I
was too tired to bother. It was a rough job."

One hand moved up to knead gently the
muscles at the nape of her neck. "All your jobs are
rough," he said thickly. "I had Ron Willet get a few
clips from your last pictures. Some of the stuff you
did scared the hell out of me." His hand was loos-
ening her ponytail and suddenly her hair tumbled
down around her shoulders in a shiny cloud. His
hands threaded through the tresses with tactile
pleasure. "So pretty. Like fragrant satin. I kept
remembering the feel of it in my hands when I was
lying in bed at night and my palms would tingle."
He chuckled huskily. "Of course that wasn't the
only portion of my anatomy that tingled."

He was stroking her hair with a gentleness
that caused her to cuddle closer to his warmth like
a kitten newly in from the cold.

"I memorized and can recall every curve and
valley of your strong silky body, but it was your
hair that I remembered the most. Your hair and
your husky, scratchy little voice that rubbed my
senses like a hand caressing me. Lord, I love your
voice."

She felt as if she were wrapped in a cloudlike
blanket of loving security. "You really had Ron go
to the trouble to get those clips?" she asked dreamily. "Why on earth did you do that?"

"That's what I asked myself. I was busy as hell
and working sixteen hours a day on *Venture*. I
should have been so tired when I finally got to bed
that I'd be knocked out with exhaustion." He was
winding the short wispy curls at her nape around
his finger. "Instead, I found I couldn't get to sleep
until I had my nightly fix of one Kendra Michaels."
His voice became a disgusted growl. "Hell, I didn't
even enjoy them. I couldn't see your face, your hair
was always covered with a wig, and the things you

were doing caused my guts to knot and my skin to break out in a cold sweat. The worst thing about it was that I knew you were probably taking the same kind of crazy chances at the exact moment I was looking at those damn clips." He drew a deep, shuddering breath. "No more, sweetheart. I can't take any more of it. It got so that I was even having nightmares about it and I couldn't wait until I got you here and could keep you safe."

She felt a nagging sense of unease that pierced the warm contentment she was feeling. What was he talking about? "Safe?" she asked slowly. "I don't know what you mean, Joel."

"I've made inquiries; Wendy Lynch is available to do the stunts on *Venture*," he said with a coolness that dumbfounded her. "I can fly her out from L.A. and have her on the set by day after tomorrow." He added quickly, "You won't suffer monetarily from the replacement, of course. You'll still get the fee agreed upon, plus a sizable compensatory bonus."

"Wendy Lynch," she repeated the name blankly, "doing *my* stunts?" She stiffened in his arms. "What the devil are you talking about? No one else is going to do my stunts!"

"Wendy Lynch is doing your stunts," he corrected, lifting his head to look down at her, his expression hard with determination. "Get used to the idea, Kendra. I told you what watching those clips did to me. Do you think I'm going through the hell of actually directing you while you're doing them? No way, rainbow lady."

Rainbow lady. The term stoked the embers of resentment smoldering within her. She deliberately stepped back out of his embrace, shrugging off his hold. "I believe we discussed the fallacy of you calling me that," she said through her teeth. "I'm not the insubstantial lightweight you want me to be. I guess I don't have to ask what duties you had in mind as a replacement for my legitimate work."

"I told you I'd take care of you," he said gruffly. "I wouldn't let you suffer for coming to me. What difference does it make where the money comes from as long as it makes you comfortable and keeps you from taking risks that could kill you?"

"How simplistic can you get? I wonder if you'd have the same attitude if I tried to hire *you* as some sort of sexual gigolo?"

He turned white, an odd, stunned look tautening his face. "A gigolo?" A bitter smile curved his lips. "Perhaps I'd be more understanding than you think. I believe my father was very much in demand in that role." He gestured impatiently. "But that's hardly pertinent to the situation. We're talking about you . . . and how we can keep you in one piece."

"You're wrong. We're talking about choices. *My* choices that you're trying to take away from me. Choices that you have no right to rob me of." Her voice was vibrating with the intensity of her feelings and her brown eyes were blazing. "For heaven's sake, you don't even have the excuse of caring about me. How could you care? You don't even know me. You don't know what I think or how I feel. All you know is that I have a responsive body you believe will amuse you for a while. Well, I'm worth more than that. I have value, damn you!"

"It's more," he said roughly. "Hell, do you think I react like this to every woman?" He shrugged helplessly, seeming to search for words. "I do want you. Right this moment I'm aching with it, but there's something else there, too. I have an urge to take care of you." He shook his head in frustration. "I worry about you. I may not know what you think or feel, but I *want* to know, dammit. Give me the opportunity, Kendra!"

"While I'm tucked away in your own private harem?" she asked mockingly. "I appreciate your consideration in putting me in a special category, but it would all come down to the same thing in the end. You don't have the reputation for a great deal of staying power, do you, Joel? Even if the arrangement you offered appealed to me, it would be too high-risk. We both know how competitive my profession is. And a harem would have a definitely softening effect."

"Your work can't be that important to you," Joel said tersely. "What can you get out of it besides money and some kind of perverse kick?"

"You may not regard it as a desirable occupation, but it's what I do for a living. I'm a stuntwoman and a damn good one." Her words had the rapid spate of a machine gun. "A stunt person isn't just a reckless idiot willing to take chances. He or she has to be in better shape physically than most professional athletes. Do you know that I spend three hours a day exercising just to maintain that strength? That I'm proficient on the trapeze, that I can fly a plane, drive a car, and race a motorboat with more skill than most professionals who make it their life's work. I'm an expert and, by God, I've paid my dues." She was glaring at him defiantly. "You think that my voice is sexy? Did you ever question how it got that way?"

He shook his head. "It never occurred to me it wasn't your natural voice."

"Hardly natural," she said. "When I was nineteen, a lariat slipped from my shoulders to my throat as I was being dragged by a horse. They got to me before my neck was broken but my larynx was permanently damaged. This husky little whisper is as loud as I'll ever be able to speak, Joel. I've had more broken bones and torn muscles and bruises than I can count, but through it all there's one thing that makes it worthwhile: I'm a professional, the very best I can be. I'm proud of what I am, Joel." She gazed at him questioningly. "Did you really think I'd give up that pride to be some kind of toy?"

He didn't seem to be listening, his face was even paler than before. He took a step closer, his eyes fixed with compulsive fascination on her throat. His hand reached out shakily to touch her smooth skin. "You were dragged along behind a horse by your throat?" He closed his eyes, his face betraying the sickness he felt. "God, I can almost see it happening." He opened his lids and his green eyes were blazing. "And you want me to stand by and watch that happening to you again? Hell no!"

She shook off his hand impatiently. "Hell *yes!*" she said, just as decisively. "I have a contract with Donovan, Limited, and as long as I fulfill my part of that contract, there's no way you can fire me, Joel." She drew a deep, steadying breath. "And I intend to fulfill that contract, every single gag and every extra bit that Skip will give me, including the special jump across the canyon."

"No!" His voice was softly menacing. "You won't even get within sight of that canyon jump. Not if I have to fire Skip Lowden and his whole team."

"You're bluffing, Joel. I know your reputation too well to believe you'd ever be that much of a bastard. You may be a workaholic and drive everyone around you into the ground, but you're a fair man. You'll keep the fireworks between us and not let any bystanders be hurt."

She could see his hands clench slowly at his sides and frustration tighten his lips. "Don't count on it, Kendra. You've had it all your own way in our relationship to date, but you can be sure that I'm not going to be satisfied with the status quo. I can make it easy or difficult for you on the set and I won't hesitate to put you through hell if it means getting what I want. That rough job you've just finished may seem like a rest cure by the time I've finished with you. In two weeks I'll wager you'll be very happy for me to send for Wendy Lynch to replace you."

"You'll lose, Joel. I've worked with difficult directors before. You'll just be one more," she said wearily. "Now if you don't mind, I'd appreciate it if you'd leave. I understand I'm to start work tomorrow morning and I'd like to settle in and get unpacked. Tomorrow you can throw anything you want at me, but I'm on my own time now. Good-bye, Joel."

He uttered a curse that was worse than anything she had ever heard from the boys in the stunt crew. "I won't be so easy to dismiss on the set tomorrow, Kendra," he said grimly. "I'd put off that unpacking and get a hell of a lot of rest instead. You're going to need it." The amber beads of the curtain jangled harshly as he stalked out the door.

She waited until the front door had slammed behind him before she allowed the tension to flow out of her. She was almost weak as she tottered over to the bed and sank down on the cushioned surface. Lord, she had never dreamed the meeting with Joel would be so difficult. She'd thought she'd fortified herself against him, but she had never expected him to exhibit such strange vulnerability and loving tenderness. She'd expected lust and arrogance, and his anxiety and protectiveness had caught her completely off guard. And on top of it all was the suggeston of pregnancy. Good Lord, his concern might have some foundation. No! She wouldn't accept it. She couldn't be that unlucky, not with all she had to do. It would be years before Casey would be finished with his training and equipped for a new career. She couldn't afford another responsibility on the scale a child would represent.

She squared her shoulders and sat up straighter on the bed. Why was she worrying about something that might never come to pass? Joel was obviously going to give her more than enough problems in the next weeks without her borrowing trouble. She rubbed her temples wearily, trying to ease the knotted tension. She was so tired of fighting and it had felt so wonderful to relax in Joel's arms and be petted so tenderly. She had wanted to stay there forever. But *forever* wasn't a word in Joel Damon's vocabulary, and despite his surprising gentleness earlier in their meeting, she knew he wasn't a man she could lean on for more than a moment. He had withdrawn that blessed support with brutal abruptness when she hadn't bowed to his wishes.

When it came down to the essentials, she was always alone, wasn't she? There was no reason why she should come unraveled at the thought now. Tomorrow she'd be able to fight him again. She'd be able to meet any challenge he could hurl at her after she had some rest. But right now that sluggish lassitude was creeping like molasses through her veins and those pillows looked irresistibly inviting.

It would be safe to let her guard down now for a little while and nap until Billie came back. The cushions were just as comfortable as they looked and her lids were already closing as she curled up like a weary child on the couch.

Child? Joel Damon's child would no doubt be

as enchanting a rascal as his father. She had a vision of a miniature replica of him: crisp curly hair, green sorcerer's eyes, and a smile that tugged at . . .

Five

The room was dim and shadowy; darkness showed through the gap in the curtain at the windows. The only light was a diffused glow emanating from the other room. That wasn't the only thing drifting into the room, though, she realized hazily. There was the low throb of a guitar and the haunting softness of a woman's voice. Billie's voice, she thought, as she got off the bed and headed toward the beaded curtain.

There is an island where only the south winds blow.
There is a river they say has no end.
There is a mountain whose peak has known no snow.
And there is a lover who only calls my name.
He only calls my name.

Billie was sitting cross-legged on an enormous cushion on the floor wearing a faded nightshirt with *Kiss me, I'm Irish* emblazoned in shamrock-green across the front. She looked up from her guitar and cast a quick warm smile at Kendra. "Hi, did I wake you?"

Kendra shook her head. "I only meant to nap for a while anyway. That's a very pretty folk song you were singing. I don't think I've heard it before."

"That's not surprising since I just made it up an hour ago." Billie's fingers moved caressingly over the strings. "I like to play around with composing every now and then. It's something to do when you're alone." She shrugged. "And when you're on the road, you find yourself alone more often than not."

"And you're on the road a lot?"

"I get restless," Billie said simply. She looked down at her guitar, her violet eyes far away. "You know, sometimes I feel there's something special out there waiting for me just around the corner or over the horizon. But when I get there, whatever it was has already faded away. I can catch a glimpse of it in the distance, but I can never quite touch it." She struck a soft chord. "So I try another road."

"Well, your roads certainly have some interesting twists and turns," Kendra said lightly. "Did you get Yusef settled?"

"If you could call it that. He's lying outside on our doorstep in a sleeping bag. Dave offered to put a cot in the wardrobe tent, but he wouldn't have it. He seems to think I'll be thrown into some dire peril if he's not right on top of me. I tried to get Joel to put a cot in here, but he turned me down flat. He said there was no way he was going to let a bordello bouncer become our roommate. Yusef isn't the only one who's overprotective around here."

"Yet you seem to be able to manage Joel very well from what I've seen," Kendra observed. "Have you known each other long?"

"About three months," Billie answered. "And no one 'manages' Joel Damon. The only reason he sometimes listens to me is because we're friends. We liked each other from the minute he picked me up on the highway one day. Sometimes it happens that way."

"He picked you up?"

"Well, not exactly the way that sounds," Billie said with a grin. She put her scratched and battered guitar aside. "Drag up a cushion and I'll tell you all about it." She suddenly snapped her fingers. "I almost forgot, you must be starved. I brought you a thermos of soup and a packet of crackers from the commissary tent at dinner time. They're on the brass table over there. I really should have awakened you but you were sleeping so deeply, I thought probably you needed rest more than food."

"I did." Kendra found the thermos, plastic spoon, and crackers and returned to where Billie was sitting. She nudged a scarlet cushion a bit closer with her toe and sank down across from her. "Thanks, Billie. I am a little hungry." She unscrewed the top of the thermos. "Now, tell me how Joel picked you up."

"My motorcycle broke down on a highway in Oregon and I was thumbing a ride to the nearest gas station when this sinfully gorgeous Mercedes slinked to a stop. Joel proceeded to read me the riot act on the dangers of hitchhiking and then he gave me the lift and ended up by offering me a job in *Venture*." She smiled, reminiscing. "I thought he was just giving me a line, but he showed me his ID and persuaded me to go on to Michael Donovan's film colony at Twin Pines with him until I made up my mind. I didn't really take much persuading. I had just left the Rainbow People and I didn't have a definite destination in mind anyway."

Kendra's eyes widened in shock. "The Rainbow people?"

Billie's expression looked shrewd. "How very odd that you and Joel should have the same reaction," she said softly. "It's an Indian tribe whose lands are situated near the Puget Sound in Washington. They have an Indian name which is a real tongue twister so most people just call them the Rainbow People. I lived with them for six months before I met Joel on that highway in Oregon."

Rainbows again. She seemed destined to be reminded of that night. Kendra's eyes dropped to the rich broth she was spooning from the thermos. "So Joel talked you into taking the part," she prompted.

Billie nodded. "I tried to tell him I couldn't act, but he said it didn't matter. The role was practically all action anyway and what he really needed was my face. He said it was a face that people would care about. With a role that has as many cliffhangers as *The Perils of Pauline*, it's very important that the audience care whether I make it across that canyon." She grinned. "Or rather, that you make it across. Anyway, I stayed at Twin Pines for a week while Joel and Michael were having their discussion. There's not a heck of a lot to do in the backwoods of Oregon, so we spent most evenings just sitting around talking, trading our life stories. You become close pretty quickly under circumstances like those."

"I guess you do," Kendra said slowly. It was ridiculous to feel this sharp twinge of jealousy. She didn't want to know the Joel Damon with whom Billie had become friends. It was too dangerous for her. As long as she could convince herself her feelings were only physical, she was safe. "It surprises me that Joel would let anyone slip beneath the armor of cynicism he wears."

"He's not all that hard to know," Billie said, her expression earnest. "He uses cynicism to protect himself from getting hurt. He wants to give to people, but he's afraid that if he does, there will be just another betrayal."

"*Another* betrayal?"

"Who knows how many there have been in his life?" Billie's eyes were compassionate. "His childhood must have been an emotional horror story. His mother was married six times and evidently shuttled him off to private schools whenever she got the opportunity. Her father was Giles Damon, the steel tycoon, and she would never have had a child at all if he hadn't wanted an heir for the business and exerted a little pressure in the only area the bitch would feel it." Her lips tightened. "Her monthly allowance."

"Aren't you being a bit hard on her?" Kendra asked lightly. Oh Lord, she didn't want to think about Joel Damon as a vulnerable, sensitive child. A child hurting and alone, who would run away to a Norman fortress to draw strength from its ancient permanence. "Perhaps she actually wanted a child herself."

Billie shook her head. "She made no bones about the fact she was coerced into having Joel. She thought it was wildly amusing to tell how she'd researched bloodlines to find just the right stud who would fulfill her father's requirements. She finally chose an Italian prince who was making a very luxurious living as a gigolo on the French Riviera. They went through a marriage ceremony to legitimize the union and Joel was born seven months later. The prince was then paid off handsomely and divorced." Billie smiled grimly. "Oh yes, she kept the title. She told everyone it was the only thing she'd gotten out of the marriage that was worth anything. With a background like that can you blame Joel for not wanting to get close to anyone?"

The gigolo. Joel had looked as if she'd struck him when she had innocently thrown that taunt at him. The pain on his face had been stark and raw before he had covered it with a sarcastic expression. Kendra suddenly couldn't take it anymore. He was becoming too real and human with every word Billie spoke. She had to keep him one-dimensional if she was to come out of this with her heart whole and emotionally intact.

She jumped to her feet. "I think I'd better get to bed if I'm going to be any good at all tomorrow," she said hurriedly as she screwed the top back on the thermos and folded the cellophane around the remaining crackers. "I have to be on the set at six." She strode across the room and put both items back on the little brass table. "I'm afraid I didn't ask which bed was mine before I just plopped."

"It doesn't matter, use either one." Billie picked up her guitar again. "Will it bother you if I play for a little while? I'm something of an insomniac."

"No problem. I sleep like a log."

"So I noticed." Billie's fingers stroked the strings lovingly. "You looked so exhausted that I was a little worried. Are you sure you're up to working tomorrow?"

"I'm sure." As Kendra moved briskly toward the bedroom, she threw the other woman a grin over her shoulder. "Haven't you heard? We stunt people are as tough as old leather."

"Try it again, Kendra." Joel's voice was silky smooth and absolutely expressionless. Kendra gritted her teeth to keep back the exclamation of pure fury she wanted to hurl at the stone-faced monster lolling carelessly in the camera's hoist some twenty feet above her. She had rolled down that bloody incline *five* times and Joel still wasn't ready to film it. She sat up and dusted off the knees of her jeans and meticulously straightened the copper curls of her wig. She would *not* complain and give Joel the satisfaction of knowing that his treatment was getting to her. She'd roll down that hill a hundred times if his august lordship decreed. She had taken all the punishment he had handed out to her in the past two weeks and she could keep on for as long as he could dish it out.

It couldn't go on like this forever. Joel was taking too much time filming her stunts and he was far too professional to let the budget suffer to indulge his own personal quirks.

"Are you okay?" Skip Lowden asked quietly as he reached down a hand to pull her to her feet. His gray eyes were as cool as ever but there was a flicker of concern in their depths. His hands ran over her hips and ribs impersonally. "The padding's holding all right?"

"Fine," she said curtly. "I have more padding than an end for the Los Angeles Rams, and it seems that I'm going to need every bit of it."

"It looks that way." Skip took her arm and was striding with her up the hill. "You're keeping loose, but I noticed on that last roll you forgot to tuck your left arm underneath you. Watch it or you could end up with a broken arm."

"I will." She hadn't been aware of the slip but she had no doubt it had happened if Skip said so. She had been tired and upset, but a lack of concentration was not only unprofessional, it could kill her. "It won't happen again, Skip."

"Just thought I'd mention it," Skip said absently. "Like I said, you're looking good." He paused a moment, oddly hesitant for someone so self-assured. "I can't take the heat off you, Kendra. I'd like to, but he's not violating any safety guidelines. In fact, when it comes to the risky gags, he's being almost too careful. He's made them in one take every time." He frowned. "And some of those shots were pretty marginal. Any other director might have had you do a repeat."

"Oh, he's a great one for repeats." They had reached the crest of the hill and she turned to face him, her expression grim. "Just ask me. I'm a living testament to his passion for repeats." She shook her head resignedly. "I know there's nothing you can do, Skip. How can you fault a director for having too many run-throughs? If I petitioned the Screen Actors Guild, they'd think I was crazy. The complaints are always on the other side of the scale."

Skip nodded. "They probably wouldn't believe any charge of harassment anyway. Damon's reputation for fairness is too well founded." He seemed puzzled. "That's why I can't understand what the hell is happening. I've worked with him before and he's been damn good to everyone on the team. Hell, most of the time I not only respect but actually like the man."

That was an impressive accolade for a man who was as fiercely protective of his team as Skip. If Joel hadn't been putting her through all the fires of hell, she knew she too could have liked the man she'd grown to know in the last two weeks. In every aspect of directing that didn't concern her personally, he was absolutely fair and sensitive to the needs of the actors and the crew he was working with. He gave as much as he demanded. And, if he was the workaholic she had accused him of being, still he had the brilliance and enthusiasm to inspire that same desire for perfection in the people around him.

She'd also discovered he had a wry sense of humor that occasionally destroyed the barrier of cynical reserve and revealed his almost boyish sense of fun. The first time she had seen that spark of mischief on his face was when he'd been joking with Billie. She had felt an odd tugging at her heart. Perhaps it was fortunate that she had been too angry with him most of the time to let that charisma seep through her guard.

Skip's eyes narrowed speculatively. "I don't suppose you have any idea why he has it in for you?"

"Does it matter?" she asked evasively. She checked the pins that held her wig in place and tucked the blue tails of her shirt more snugly into her jeans. "The only important thing is for me to survive it. It will all be over in another few days anyway. After this I've only got the horse chase through the desert," she paused deliberately, "and the jump across the canyon."

A rare smile tugged at Skip's lips. "You're pushing, Ken." The smile abruptly disappeared. "Damon paid me a visit last week and told me that I wasn't to give you that special under any circumstances."

Kendra tensed. "And?"

"I told him I'd give it to anyone I damn well pleased. No one tells me how to run my shop." Seeing the hope that suddenly lit her face he continued quickly, "That doesn't mean you've got it, Ken. I still haven't made a decision. I'll let you know after the horse chase." He touched his index finger lightly to her cheek. "You've done a good job so far, Ken. Hang in there." Then he wheeled and strode rapidly down the hill. He turned his head to call back over his shoulder, "And keep that left arm tucked under."

She laughed and nodded. "Right." She was suddenly buoyantly optimistic, her former weariness and discouragement completely gone. She waved mockingly at Joel on the hoist. "Ready, Mr. Damon?"

"Whenever you are, Kendra." Joel's voice was equally mocking.

She dropped to the ground, her gaze on Joel's sardonic face, half hidden by sunglasses. "Let's go for it!"

She drew a deep breath and launched herself forward, curling into a loose pliant ball, carefully keeping her arms tucked in. It was a bone-jarring tumble even with her padding and the special preparations that had been made to the earth on her charted path down the hill, but the momentum of her descent was so swift that she wasn't aware of any danger until she heard Skip's strident yell.

"Straighten out! For God's sake, straighten out, Kendra!"

Something was wrong, she thought with a cold rush of fear. Then it was too late for any thought at all because the ground beneath her was suddenly much harder and she felt sharp pain as the sleeve of her shirt ripped and the soft skin of her upper arm was exposed to the rocky terrain.

Rocks! There shouldn't be any rocks on this specially prepared path down the slope. Then she felt a hot wrenching agony in her lower back that blanked out all other sensations as well as thought. For several seconds she wasn't even aware that she had reached the bottom of the hill and was lying in a limp heap a full five yards from the target area.

Skip reached her first. "Don't move," he

ordered curtly, falling to his knees beside her. His hands were moving over her arms and legs swiftly. "Where does it hurt?"

"My back," she said dazedly, "and my arm. What happened, Skip?"

"Your body wasn't in line with the path," he said absently. "You know even an inch or so slant can change the direction of the roll. You were only halfway down the hill when you catapulted off the path." He glanced up reprovingly. "You should have checked your angle before you launched."

She knew that, she thought crossly. She always checked the angle as a matter of course. But she hadn't this time, damn it. She had been too busy gawking like a moon-eyed teenager at Joel Damon. How stupid could you get?

"Do you think anything's broken?" Skip asked. "Shall I get a stretcher?"

She shook her head adamantly. "I just had the breath knocked out of me and wrenched my back a little. Give me a minute and I'll be fine. Help me to sit up, will you?"

HIs arm was immediately around her shoulders and he was slowly levering her into a sitting position. "Yell if there's any pain and I'll stop."

There was pain but less than she'd expected, she realized with relief. The weak ligaments hadn't torn again as she had feared and the pain was probably only due to severe bruising. "It's okay," she said. "After I get my arm patched up, I'll be able to do it again."

"The hell you will." Joel pushed through the circle of people surrounding her and dropped to his knees beside her. His green eyes were blazing in his pale face. "I think you've done enough damage for one day." He turned to Skip. "Does she need a doctor?"

"I don't think so," Skip answered. "It's probably just general bruising. Give her a couple hours and you'll be able to get the take."

"Screw the take," Joel said succinctly. "She's not working any more today."

With one arm under her knees and the other around her back, he eased her away from Skip's hold. "I'll take care of her. Tell Ron we're postponing the scene indefinitely and to shoot around it." Then he was lifting and carrying her toward the jeep that was parked with the other vehicles at the edge of the clearing. She had been too surprised to protest at first, but as he placed her carefully in the passenger seat of the jeep she snapped out of her bemusement.

"This isn't necessary, you know," she said coolly. "I'll be perfectly able to complete the take after I clean up the scratch on my arm and change my shirt. I know you don't want to lose any shooting time just because I blew the run-through."

"Shut up," Joel grated through set teeth as he slipped into the driver's seat and put the jeep in gear. "How could you know anything? You've got to be the most stubborn, stupidest woman on the face of the earth." He was gunning the accelerator and tearing down the dirt road toward the village. "Just look at you. You're dirty and bleeding; probably every inch of your body is bruised and battered. You've been rolling down that lousy hill half the afternoon at the command of a man who could tell you to do it indefinitely." His fist slammed against the steering wheel. "And you'd do it, dammit. You'd do it for as long as you were told to do it."

"What the devil are you so angry about?" she blazed back at him. "You're the one giving the orders, remember? I merely do what the great god in the director's chair decrees."

"You didn't have to obey those decrees. You

could have opted out at any time. If you had any sense at all, you would have done just that."

"I'm sure you would have liked that very much, wouldn't you, Joel? That would have proved how right you were about me. Simply one more weak, clinging female willing to give up her independence and lean on your big strong shoulders. Sorry to disappoint you." She found she was trembling and wrapped her arms around herself. "I don't know why you're so upset. It was just another stunt and not even a very dangerous one at that. On film it's going to look like an amusing romp when Billie tumbles down that hill and then bounds to her feet with a John Williams march blaring in the background."

"An amusing romp," he echoed through clenched teeth. "I think you'd better shut up, Kendra. One more word out of you and I may do more damage to you than that bitch of a hill."

"I still think you're being absurd to cancel the shooting when I can perfectly well—"

"Kendra." Her name was spoken with an icy menace that caused her to subside reluctantly. It was obvious that Joel was furious and she was in no shape to fight him at the moment. She had better save her strength to fight off the weakness that was attacking her limbs. It was only reaction. She'd be better any minute now. Just breathe deeply and get control of your muscles, she told herself.

They were both silent for the rest of the way to the village. It was only when Joel pulled to a stop in front of a large trailer that served him as an office as well as quarters that she spoke.

"You're not taking me to the first aid tent?"

"I said I'd take care of you." Joel was out of the jeep and unlocking the front door of the trailer. He turned and before she could get out of the jeep, he scooped her up and carried her up the stairs. "I want to make sure you're all right myself. I wouldn't put it past you to try to hide a couple of broken ribs just to prove what a tough broad you are." He put her down carefully on the long blue couch that took one entire wall of the living room of the trailer. "Now, sit there while I get some bandades and antiseptic. I don't want you to move a muscle, understand?"

He didn't wait for an answer but strode swiftly toward the back of the trailer, pausing a moment to close the front door on the way.

She wished he hadn't done that. With the door open, the afternoon sunshine had helped to relieve the coldness of the air conditioning in the trailer. Now she couldn't seem to stop shivering. She stared unseeingly at the portable movie screen across from the couch, trying desperately to control that sign of weakness before Joel came back.

"What the hell?" Joel's voice was rough with exasperation as he appeared beside her with a metal first aid box, a cloth, and a basin of water in his hand. He set them on the floor and knelt before her. "You're shaking like a malaria victim. I thought you said you were all right?"

"I am all right," she said quickly. "It's just that the air conditioning is turned up so high that my body hasn't adjusted to it after the heat outside. Give me a minute and I'll be fine."

"If you don't shake to pieces first." He got lithely to his feet and moved swiftly to the closet across the room. In a moment he was back and wrapping a gray tweed sport coat around her shoulders. It smelled of spicy cologne and fine wool and was blessedly warm, but instinctively she tried to slip it off and return it to him.

"No," she protested. "I'll get blood on it."

"Sit still," he said tersely as he dropped down

on his knees before her once again. He opened the first aid box and took out a bandage, scissors, and antiseptic, and put them on the floor. Then his hands were on her shirt, rapidly unbuttoning it.

"But blood stains are very difficult—"

"I'm sure you're an expert on blood stains, but I'm not really interested." He parted the shirt to stare at her in amazement. "What in heaven's name do you have on?"

"Padding." She looked down at the thin long-sleeved vest she was wearing. "Very efficient. It's not too bulky but has a tough cushion that offers more protection than you'd think. It was developed by NASA for the astronaut program."

"Fascinating," Joel said dryly. "It can't be too tough by the look of that tear in the sleeve."

"It's not supposed to act as armor, only a cushion. I wasn't supposed to encounter any obstacles on that path!"

"I know that," he said roughly. He had finished unfastening the undervest and was carefully slipping it off her shoulders. "There wasn't supposed to be any danger to you at all on the roll. Do you think I would have had you do it over and over if I had had any idea this would happen?" He glared disgustedly at the white elastic binding he'd uncovered. "And now what the devil is this, another vest?"

She shook her head. "It's an elastic bandage to flatten my breasts. I have to wear it all the time when I'm doubling for Billie." She added quickly, "You don't have to take it off. It's wrapped around me underneath my armpits and won't get in your way when you're bandaging my arm."

But his hands were already at the fastening at her rib cage. "It comes off. It must be hellishly uncomfortable being wrapped up in that strait-jacket. Don't worry, I'm not about to be overcome by lechery. I'm feeling a hell of a lot of emotions at the moment, but lust isn't one of them." He unwound the bandage with an impersonal deftness, watching dispassionately as her naked breasts sprang to their former fullness when he freed them. "What a criminal waste to do that to them." Then his hands were at the pins that secured her wig and a moment later his fingers were combing through her chestnut hair as it tumbled about her shoulders. "That's better. I was beginning to wonder if I was ever going to come to the end of this camouflage." His hands were wringing out the warm soapy cloth in the basin and he gently began to wash her face and throat.

It was very soothing sitting there as he stroked the wash cloth over her breasts and stomach before he slipped the tweed jacket from her shoulders. She started to shiver again as the cool air touched her damp skin. "I'll be through here in just a minute and get you something to slip on," he said as he quickly washed her shoulders and then her arms. "This cut isn't as bad as I thought. When I first saw the blood I thought you were really hurt. It's not much more than a scratch."

"I told you there wasn't any need to delay the shooting." She watched as he put antiseptic on the jagged cut and then applied the bandage. "You've got the shot all set up and there's no sense wasting it. If you'll drive me back, we can still get the take this afternoon."

"Don't you ever give up?" He was drying her with a soft terry towel. "The only place you're going is back to your cottage to rest. Tomorrow you'll probably be so stiff you won't be able to move."

"All the more reason to get the take today," she insisted stubbornly as she watched him walk to the closet and slip a collarless long-sleeved black shirt from a hanger. "We both know that it was my carelessness that caused the accident and I won't have anybody saying I held up production just to pamper a few bruises."

He muttered something obscene as he returned to stand before her. He carefully put her arms into the sleeves of the shirt. "Look, will you just drop it?" He knelt before her, his hands at the buttons at the bottom of the shirt. "You're shaking so much you can hardly sit up and you're still trying to prove you're some kind of superwoman." He wasn't looking at her, his gaze fixed with intentness on the buttons he was fastening. "You don't have to be so blasted strong twenty-four hours out of every day." His voice was oddly husky. "Let someone help you once in a while, for heaven's sake. Let *me* help you, Kendra."

Her gaze was fixed on the hands buttoning the black shirt and she saw to her amazement that she wasn't the only one who was trembling. Joel's long slender fingers were shaking so badly he barely managed to fasten the two bottom buttons. She noticed for the first time that he was sickly pale. "Joel," she said hesitatingly, her eyes dark with concern. "What's wrong? Are you ill?"

He drew a deep shuddering breath, still not looking at her. "You might say that. I feel pretty sick at the moment anyway." He gave up the struggle with the buttons and rested his forehead against her breast, his eyes closed. "Oh Lord, do I ever feel sick."

Her hands went up instinctively to tangle in the dark crispness of his hair, holding him to her protectively. "Joel, I don't understand . . ."

He nestled his head against her like a weary little boy, pushing aside the open shirt to press his cheek to the warmth of her bare breasts. "You're so soft, so womanly. I had almost forgotten in the last two weeks." His lips brushed lightly over one gentle rise. "I never meant to hurt you, Kendra. As God is my witness, I never wanted to cause you a moment's pain or danger. Please believe me."

"I believe you." Kendra's throat was clogged as she tenderly stroked his hair. "Of course I believe you, Joel."

"I don't know how you can." His cheek was slightly rough as he rubbed against her breast with a movement that was more affectionate than sensual. "Not after what I've put you through in the last couple of weeks, what I did to you today. And you're wrong, it wasn't your fault we didn't get that take today. It was mine. Everything that happened to you today was my fault and if you had been seriously injured, that would have been my fault, too." He laughed mirthlessly. "I tried to tell myself I was doing it for your own good, to show you that the kind of punishment you're subjected to isn't worth the bucks you get for your work. But I knew inside that was pure unadulterated bull. You were right. I wanted to prove you less than you are. I wanted you to surrender. Not only because that would keep you safe, but it would keep me safe as well. You were already possessing my body; I didn't want to give you a chance at taking over my soul as well. Can you understand that?"

Oh yes, she could understand that. His words reflected a mirror image of the struggle she had been going through herself since that night at his House of Rainbows. The realization that the battle had been shared by the man she was holding in her arms brought her a sudden feeling of kinship, a lessening of defensive antagonism. His simple honesty was a weapon against which she had no defense. "You were only doing your job," she said with an unexplainable desire to comfort him. "I realize that."

He raised his head to look at her and his eyes

were dark with pain. "You're lying. You knew what I was doing to you. I could see it in your face every time I pushed you a little bit more. Sometimes I could see how exhausted you were and I'd want to yell cut, then run out and scoop you up and protect you against all the dragons in your world." His lips curved bitterly. "But how could I do that when I was one of those dragons myself? So I pushed you even harder and watched you lose weight, saw the circles appear beneath your eyes." His finger reached out to touch the hollow of her cheek. "I watched the strain grow in you until it was an aching pain inside me." He shook his head in bewilderment. "Because by that time I felt as if we were linked somehow so that I could actually tell what you were feeling. Lord, Freud would have had a field day with me for the last two weeks."

"You could have stopped at any time, you know," she said with a wry smile. "I guarantee I wouldn't have objected to a cessation of hostilities if you'd cared to hoist a truce flag."

He shook his head, "I couldn't do that." His finger traced a gentle path to her lower lip. "Because you see, I wasn't doing what I set out to do. I was losing ground every day, with every moment I spent with you. You were coming closer all the time and I couldn't let that happen. I was watching more than your exhaustion and discomfort; I was watching you *endure*. I was watching your strength and determination, your quiet friendliness with everyone on the set." He frowned. "Everyone but me. God, I was jealous when I'd see you laughing and joking with Billie. Your face would light up and suddenly you'd look as young and carefree as a kid. Then you'd look at me and you'd close up again. I didn't know why, but it hurt, dammit. Everything you did and said hurt me."

The mirror again. "I had to close up," she said. "I couldn't let you hurt me. My life is difficult enough without my becoming vulnerable to a man who won't see me as I am."

"That's what I'm trying to say," he said. "I fought it like hell, but it hasn't done any good. You're not a rainbow lady to me anymore." His eyes were grave. "You're real to me now. More real than anyone I've ever known. And I'm not fighting anymore, Kendra. After I saw you lying at the bottom of the hill, I knew I had lost that particular battle." He framed her face with hands, and they were magically gentle. "I'll never hurt you again. I only want to show you that I'm not quite the bastard I've been acting. Will you let me do that?"

"It wouldn't make any difference," she said haltingly. "A relationship between us isn't going to pan out. There are too many factors working against us."

"I don't know about you, but I don't think I have a choice any longer." His eyes were quietly compelling. "I'm not asking you to move in with me. I think I know you well enough to realize you'd be too wary to consider it." His lips twisted. "Surprisingly enough, I find I don't even want that right now." His gaze dropped to the cleavage revealed by the open shirt. "I can't give any guarantee how long my celibate mood will last, however. I think you know how much I desire you." He smiled slightly as he noticed the unmistakable response to that casual glance and bent to brush his lips against the taut pink tip. "And you desire me too, don't you, love? I don't know how long either of us is going to hold out, but I think we ought to try." His hands left her face to finish buttoning her shirt. "Sex has a way of confusing issues and I want everything between us to be crystal clear from now on." The last button was fastened and he sat back on his heels. "You haven't answered me."

There was a flicker of anxiety in his eyes that melted any remaining protest she might have made. It was probably not wise, but she knew what her answer was going to be. He had touched her on too many levels for her to do anything else.

"You'll have to clarify the question," she teased. "All you've told me so far is what you *don't* want to do."

She could feel the tension ebb out of him. "If clarification is what you need, I'll be glad to oblige." He leaned forward and took her carefully in his arms and held her for a long, peaceful moment. Then he lifted her chin to look into her eyes. "I want you to let me be with you. I'll postpone the stunts for a week but I still want you with me on the set. I want you by my side every minute we can squeeze into the day. I want to hold you in my arms like this whenever we get the chance, and when the opportunity presents itself, I want to kiss you." His lips covered hers with a softness and tenderness that was so moving she could feel warmth unfold down deep inside her. He lifted his head. "Like that. We'll leave the rest up to time and the winds of fate. Okay?"

"Okay," she said softly. She wasn't cold anymore despite the fact that she was still trembling. That glowing warmth was spreading through her like rays of sunlight. "We'll leave it up to fate."

He kissed her once more with slow, lingering tenderness. "Which will be a departure for both of us, my very pragmatic lady." He drew a deep, shaky breath and released her. "Now I think it's time I took you back to your cottage and let you get to bed." He grimaced. "And I'll go back to the set and see about rearranging the shooting schedule for next week." He held up his hand as she started to protest. "It's worth it," he murmured. "That's the way I want it." He pulled her to her feet, his arm slipping around her waist possessively. He suddenly frowned. "You're still shivering."

"It's nothing," she said lightly. "I'll have Yusef make me a cup of tea when I get home and I'll be fine."

"Yusef?" His face cleared. "I had forgotten Billie's surprise package. I gather you're not having any problems with him underfoot?"

"It wouldn't matter if we were," she said lightly. "Where Billie goes, so goes her faithful St. Bernard, complete with rescue brandy and very sharply pointed teeth. He's appointed himself our *majordomo*. He keeps the cottage clean, washes our clothes, he's even decided that the commissary food isn't nourishing enough for Billie, so he cooks at least one meal a day." She laughed. "I'm just on the outer fringe of all this devotion and I still feel smothered."

He chuckled. "I can imagine how our little gypsy is reacting. I suppose he's no longer sleeping on your doorstep?"

Kendra shook her head with an answering grin. "Billie moved his bedroll into a corner of the living room the night after I arrived. She was afraid he might catch cold. I'm not sure who's adopting whom. It turns out Yusef knew some English and now she's making him speak it all the time. I think she's trying to prepare him for a vocation other than bordello bouncer. She may hit you for work for him any day now."

"It wouldn't surprise me," Joel said dryly. "I just hope she doesn't have *my* job in mind for him." He opened the door and helped her down the steps. "At the moment I'd rather he be on hand to keep an eye on you."

Six

    "I won't stand for it," Dirk Danford bellowed. "Do you hear me, Damon?"

    Kendra and Billie looked up, startled, from where they were sitting a few yards from the cameras and lights of the set. The dark-haired Adonis of a million women's daydreams was looking less than appealing at the moment with his face flushed an apoplectic scarlet and his lips compressed in a tight line as he faced Joel and waved a scrap of black satin material in front of his face. Kendra shook her head wonderingly as she saw Joel turn away from the discussion he'd been having with the light director to gaze at Danford with glacier cool eyes. She'd discovered in the past weeks that Billie was right about the actor being a conceited lecher, but she hadn't thought he was a complete fool. People didn't talk to Joel Damon in that tone of voice, not even superstars.

    "Joel," Dirk continued, "you'll have to get to the bottom of this or I walk."

"I think not," Joel said with utmost softness, but suddenly the atmosphere was several degrees cooler. "I believe even you're more intelligent than that, Dirk. I have the final love scene between you and Brenna to film today and I want it in the can by evening. After that you can do whatever you damn well please." He glanced at the scrap of material in Danford's hand. "I gather that has something to do with this nonsense. What the hell is it?"

"My shorts." Danford shook the underwear out dramatically. "Look at this. It will take me hours to get out all the knots and every pair in my dressing room has been sabotaged just like this."

"Black satin jockey shorts?" Kendra whispered.

"Hasn't he told you? Dirk's a sex god," Billie murmured.

"And that's not all," Dirk ranted on. "Two days ago someone chained shut the door of my trailer. It took me an hour of pounding and shouting before anyone came and got me out."

"As popular as Dirk is around here, it was lucky it wasn't a month," Billie said sotto voce.

"And what about what happened yesterday to my shoes? How could one of every pair of shoes I possess simply disappear?" He lifted his foot. "Look at me. One tennis shoe and one moccasin. I look utterly ridiculous."

Kendra couldn't help it; she began to chuckle. The sound immediately brought the irate actor's attention to the corner where she was sitting with Billie. Dirk's frown took on a new dimension as he spotted Billie sprawled in the chair beside Kendra.

"You!" He stalked over to glare accusingly at her. "You know something about this, don't you? Who did it?"

"Poltergeists?" Billie offered, blinking up at him innocently.

"Not likely," Danford bit out through clenched teeth. "You're finding all this very amusing aren't you, Billie?" His hand delved into the pocket of his robe and brought out several sheets of memo paper. "I suppose you don't know anything about these either?" He scowled as he read the first one. "As you lust, so shall you reap." He read another one. "Thou shalt not covet thy producer's wife." He crumpled the notes and threw them on the floor. "I've been finding them in my dressing room, pinned to the pillow on my bed. I even stepped out of the shower stall yesterday and found one taped to the shower door."

Kendra suddenly darted Billie a suspicious glance. What had Billie said about Brenna needing a little help? Oh Lord, poltergeists, indeed!

"Well, if the shoe fits," Billie drawled. She covered her mouth with her hand. "Oops! Sorry. I forgot you were a bit sensitive on the subject of shoes."

Joel was beside them now. "If you're through making accusations and disrupting my set, I'd appreciate it if you'd occupy yourself elsewhere, Dirk." His voice dripped sarcasm. "Preferably learning your lines. You blew them twice this morning."

"But I saw that big Arab of hers skulking outside my dressing room," Dirk sputtered. "I know she—"

"*Now*, Dirk," Joel said with soft menace.

With a violent curse Danford turned on his heel and strode furiously toward his dressing room.

Joel turned to Billie, his eyes narrowed. "I don't suppose you know a thing about all this, brat?"

"Who, me?" Billie asked, her eyes widening. "Do I look like the kind of girl who would invade a man's privacy while he was in the shower?" She grinned impishly. "Though come to think about it, I might be the only woman on the set who'd be safe alone with a nude Dirk Danford."

"I'm not at all sure that paraphrasing the Bible wouldn't be considered blasphemy," Kendra said, her eyes twinkling.

"Billie, I don't know what you're up to, but I won't have you unnecessarily upsetting that ass," Joel said impatiently. "I have a picture to finish."

Billie jumped to her feet and squeezed Joel's arm affectionately. "Don't worry, Joel," she said soothingly as she turned to leave. "The man obviously has no stamina. It will be over before you know it."

Joel watched Billie walk away, exasperation warring with amusement in his expression. "*What* will be over before I know it?"

"I think it would be safer not to ask," Kendra said dryly.

"You're probably right." He dropped into the seat Billie had just vacated. "That's all I need, a personality conflict on the set." He grimaced. "And with Billie involved, it will probably escalate into a major brouhaha."

"You can handle it," Kendra said quietly. In the past week she had practically lived in his pocket and she had discovered Joel could handle almost anything. He seemed to thrive on problems that would drive most directors into a rage. "I think you enjoy these little challenges."

"Yes, I'll handle it," he said absently, his hand covering hers. "But I could do with a few less challenges at the moment. This week hasn't worked out the way I hoped. I've scarcely been able to talk to you, much less anything else."

"Anything else?" Kendra asked with a teasing smile.

The sexual tension had been growing steadily between them in the last few days, aggravated by the intensity of the schedule that kept them apart. Yet in a way she'd been glad of this hiatus. She'd enjoyed the casual intimacy of the occasional warm smile Joel gave her as he looked up from the storyboard or returned to the camera after setting up a bit of action. She liked the way he'd come over during a break to where she was quietly watching and just take her hand and hold it with calm affection. Sometimes he talked about the day's shooting; sometimes he said nothing if he were trying to solve one of the myriad problems he faced every day. She even liked the way he would brush her cheek with an absentminded kiss when he left her to return to the fray. It was a lovingly intimate and commonplace gesture that a husband might make toward a wife of a dozen years.

"You know what I mean." His green eyes were intent on her lips. "I haven't even had a chance to touch you in the last three days." His thumb caressed her inner wrist. "And I want to touch you, Kendra. I *need* it."

She felt her lips tingle under that look and she pulled her gaze away from him with some difficulty. "You've been very busy. The picture is almost finished now, isn't it?"

He nodded. "This is the last dialogue scene we're shooting this afternoon." His hand tightened on hers as his voice deepened with impatience. "And then I'll have to go over the rushes tonight to see if anything has to be reshot before I let Brenna and Dirk leave Sedikhan tomorrow." He scowled. "There'd better not be any. Michael Donovan doesn't like Brenna doing these bedroom scenes when he's not on the set. He sure as hell wouldn't appreciate any retakes." He leaned over and dropped a light kiss on Kendra's forehead. "Tomorrow," he promised as he got to his feet. "Even if we have to work until three in the morning to get the scene right, we'll have some time together tomorrow." He turned and walked quickly toward the number two camera beside the king-size bed that was the central focus on the set.

Maybe, Kendra thought wryly as she watched Joel, totally absorbed as he talked to the cameraman. Perfection couldn't always be regimented and Joel was definitely a perfectionist.

"Hi, is it okay if I sit down or will Joel be coming back?"

Kendra glanced up to see Brenna Donovan smiling down at her.

"Not until the scene is over and from what he said that may mean hours." She genuinely liked Brenna. Though Joel's marathon schedule hadn't given her much opportunity to get to know the actress, she found her to be not only a dedicated professional, but a warm and charming woman as well. She looked enchantingly lovely in a yellow chiffon negligee, her rich brown hair a shiny contrast to the delicate primrose shade. "You look absolutely beautiful, Brenna."

Brenna made a face as she sat down. "Well, at least the gown itself isn't see-through," she said. "I'd hate to think Dirk was getting a free show every time he looked at me."

"You're nervous about doing this scene coming up?"

"A little," Brenna admitted, her eyes fixed apprehensively on the bed. "Michael's always been here before when I had to do something like this. I guess he thought it would be all right since Joel is directing. He has a great deal of respect for Joel."

"Billie said you were having trouble with Dirk."

"That's putting it mildly." Brenna sighed.

"The man has as many hands as an octopus and you can't believe his conceit! I've been dreading this particular scene all week. You'd be surprised what can go on under those covers even with thirty or forty people looking on."

"You could tell Joel," Kendra suggested. "He can't do anything to help you if you don't complain."

Brenna's lips tightened determinedly. "No, I can't rely on Michael and Joel always to work out my problems. I'll handle Dirk myself."

"Just so it's not the other way around," Kendra said with a grin. "I hear your husband would react very forcefully if that happened."

A tender smile curved Brenna's lips. "Yes, he would. But then Michael is very forceful about most things." Her brown eyes were wistful. "Great heavens, I miss the man! I can hardly wait to get on that plane for London tomorrow. This is the first separation we've had since we've been married. And long-distance calls every night just don't cut it. He wanted to bundle the kids onto an airplane last week and bring them with him to Sedikhan. I almost wish I'd let him do it."

"You have children?"

Brenna nodded. "Randy and Janine. They're usually with us on location, but we thought it might be a little primitive here in Sedikhan, so we decided it would be better if they stayed in London with Michael."

Kendra felt a swift surge of sympathy and a little of Billie's indignation. Brenna was having a very unhappy time of it without her family and didn't deserve the added problem of Dirk Danford to plague her.

"Oh, oh," Brenna said gloomily. "Here comes Mr. Macho himself." She watched balefully as Danford approached the set, wearing the same wine-velvet robe he had worn earlier. She stood up and tightened the belt of her robe. "Wish me luck. I'm probably going to need it."

Brenna was gone for only a few moments when Billie plopped down beside Kendra and lazily stretched out her jean-clad legs. "Brenna really looks terrific, doesn't she?" she asked cheerfully. "You'll notice she doesn't have big bazooms either. It's almost enough to give me hope."

"So you decided it was safe to come back," Kendra teased. "You think Joel's going to be too occupied to cross-examine you?"

Billie nodded, her gaze shifting from Joel, to Brenna, to Dirk. There was an anticipatory gleam in the violet depths of her eyes. "Yep, I figured I could stay out of Joel's way here and still have a ringside seat for the great unveiling."

"Unveiling?"

"Just watch and see," Billie said. "One of the extras who worked on his last picture told me that Dirk pulled a tricky stunt that would have rivaled one of yours. I'm just betting he'll do the same thing today. The man is sinfully unoriginal."

Kendra gave her a puzzled glance before turning back to watch the action on the set.

Brenna was slipping off her negligee and getting into bed while Joel gave her a few last-minute instructions. Then Kendra's gaze wandered to the opposite side of the bed where Danford was standing and she gasped incredulously. Danford was shrugging out of the velvet robe and he was totally nude!

"What did I tell you?" Billie murmured.

There was a wave of commentary on the set. Brenna's eyes widened in shock, but Joel's registered only impatience. "For God's sake, Dirk, I told you nudity wouldn't be required for this scene. It's not going to be even close to sexually explicit. I'm shooting from the waist up."

"I know that," Dirk said with grandiose dignity. "However, I always believe in really getting into a part whenever possible." He smirked at the snickers from the crew. "I think you'll find that if I can relate, I turn in a far better performance."

"Frankly, I don't care if you wear bells on your toes and a codpiece," Joel said, obviously annoyed. "Let's just get this scene shot without any more delay." He glanced at Brenna. "If Brenna has no objections?"

Brenna's eyes were glinting angrily but her voice was cool. "I don't see why I should object to something," her gaze wandered over Danford's body, "so trivial."

This time the snickers became guffaws and Danford flushed angrily. He opened his lips to speak, but Joel turned away, carefully smothering a smile. "Good. Now that that's settled, let's get rolling. Into bed, Dirk."

"Delighted," Dirk drawled as he sat down on his side of the bed and lifted the covers. His smile was definitely feral as he slipped beneath the covers and slithered closer to Brenna. "This is what I've been waiting for ever since we started the picture."

Billie suddenly leaned forward, her face tense with excitement. "Just a little more," she urged softly. "Just a few inches more, Dirk baby." As if in compliance, Dirk gave Brenna a smoldering look à la Richard Gere, and scooted still closer to her.

Suddenly his eyes widened in horror. He let out a bellow that shook the rafters of the room and brought Joel wheeling around to face him. Danford scrambled frantically out of the bed; his hands cupped his naked buttocks like a little boy who had just been spanked. "I'm on fire! I'm burning! Dammit, don't just stand there; put it out!"

The crew just stared dumbfounded at him. He muttered a savage curse, jerked the covers from the bed, and threw them on the floor.

Misty smoke rose from the center of the bed, and Kendra thought there really was a fire. Then she spied a crystalline gleam within an oilcloth cradle, the whole covered by a sheet of plastic wrap.

"Dry ice," she gasped. "Billie, you didn't?" She turned but the chair next to hers was empty. Then she caught the glint of sunlight on copper curls as Billie slipped out the door. Billie, very obviously, had. And as Kendra's gaze went back to the disaster the imp had left in her wake, she suddenly broke into whoops of laughter.

She wasn't alone. The entire cast and crew were convulsed with mirth and Danford's expression of indignation only added fuel to the gales of laughter rocking the room. Brenna was lying back on the pillows, her body shaking helplessly, and Joel was grinning from ear to ear.

"Where is she?" Danford raved, his eyes searching wildly about the room. "Where's Billie Callahan? I'm going to cut her heart out."

Joel made a massive effort and managed to banish the grin from his face before he strode forward. He retrieved Danford's robe and handed it to him. "I think the lady's done a flit," he said lightly. "And there's no use going after her unless you want to take on her very lethal bodyguard. I think your best course of action is to go back to your dressing room and cool off." Then as the room once more rocked with laughter, Joel's lips twitched uncontrollably. "Sorry, that was purely unintentional, I assure you."

"I bet," Danford said sourly. He was muttering

obscenities as he shrugged into his velvet robe and stomped off the set.

"That's it," Joel called, "we're wrapping for today. There's no way I could get a performance out of Danford until he has time to repair the damage done to his self-esteem. Everybody be back on the set at six A.M. tomorrow." He turned to Brenna and helped her from the bed. "Sorry, Brenna, I know you wanted to fly out to London tomorrow."

"It's almost worth it," Brenna said, smiling. "Lord, I wish the camera had been rolling. I'd give anything to have a black market tape of Dirk jumping out of that bed like a scalded cat." She put on her negligee and patted Joel's arm. "Don't be too hard on Billie. It may mean an afternoon's shooting lost, but I'd be willing to bet we're going to see a very chastened Dirk Danford once he has time to think. Like I said, it may be worth it." She made a face. "Now I think I'd better go make a call to Michael and break the news."

She had no sooner turned away than Joel was striding toward Kendra, a slight smile lingering on his lips.

"Where on earth did Billie get that ice?" Kendra asked, still chuckling.

"Who knows?" Joel's eyes were twinkling. "She probably charmed somebody in the commissary tent." He pulled her to her feet. "But as Brenna said, it just might have been worth all the uproar. How fast can you change and be ready to go?" He propelled her toward the door.

"We're going somewhere?"

He nodded. "I suddenly have no scenes to shoot and no rushes to view." He glanced down at her and she inhaled sharply at the smoldering need she saw in his eyes. "That means I can do exactly what I want to do." He touched the curve of her cheek with a gentle fingertip. "If the lady wants to do it, too. Does she, Kendra?"

Abruptly she found it hard to breathe. There was no doubt in her mind what he meant. The sexual tension between them had been too raw and intense in the past few days to mistake. She knew that she'd been as much in a fever as Joel to be in his arms again. "Oh yes, the lady definitely wants it, too," she said softly.

"Thank heaven for that lovely clear honesty of yours! If you'd gone coy on me, I think I'd have been tempted to drag you to the nearest cave by your hair. And I want to do things right for you tonight, sweetheart. Dinner, conversation, romance, the works." He swatted her lightly on the fanny. "I'll tie up a few loose ends here and pick you up in an hour. Okay?"

"Okay." She turned and walked into the sunlit street, her steps as buoyant as her suddenly soaring spirits.

Kendra gazed at her reflection in the mirror over the washstand. As much as she could tell from the slightly distorted image, the white cotton halter dress with its fitted waist and bodice and graceful full skirt was very flattering. Its pristine white was an attractive foil for the gold of her skin and the shiny chestnut of her hair. And most of all, the dress made her feel deliciously feminine after the jeans and slacks she'd worn ever since she had arrived in Sedikhan.

And she wanted to be very feminine tonight, she thought happily as she brushed her hair into a shining cloud around her shoulders and stepped into white sling-back high heels. She felt a little of the reckless exuberance she had known that night at Joel's Rainbow Keep, but this time she knew for certain that it had nothing to do with drugs or alcohol. It was Joel Damon himself who was causing this breathless excitement. Strange that she felt no shyness or restraint about the idea of spending the night with Joel. After a lifetime of total disinterest in the physical act of lovemaking perhaps she was turning into a wanton. No, that couldn't be, for it was only Joel who could provoke the heady desire and totally incomprehensible wealth of tenderness she was feeling now.

She sprayed her pulse points lightly with Joy, snatched up a lacy white shawl, and tripped through the amber-beaded curtains, where Yusef stood by the table.

"Will you tell Billie . . ." Her voice trailed off as the room seemed to shimmer and then narrow into a dark box. She gave a frightened cry and was scarcely aware of Yusef's startled exclamation. Then his arms were around her and he was lifting and carrying her to the wooden chair by the table. He set her down with utmost gentleness and kneeled beside her, his hands holding her steady while the room whirled around her. She clutched desperately at his massive shoulders while she drew in great gasps of oxygen in an attempt to stave off that frightening darkness.

"You have need for," Yusef paused, searching for the word he wanted, "a *physician*?"

"No," Kendra said quickly. The darkness was fading rapidly now and there was no way she was going to let anything interfere with this evening with Joel. "I was only a little dizzy for a moment. I've probably been working too hard lately." But she hadn't worked at all for the last week and she had had another little dizzy spell like this only a few days ago, she remembered. It had been much lighter and she hadn't come close to fainting as she had this time, but she had definitely suffered the same vertigo. No, she wouldn't think about it. She was feeling better every minute.

She sat up straight in the chair and smiled with determined cheerfulness at Yusef, who clearly was worried. "I'm fine now," she announced as she brushed a lock of hair from her eyes. "Sorry to have worried you. You can let me go, Yusef."

He reluctantly removed the support of his arms. "You are certain?" he asked, a frown on his face. His keen gaze flicked for an instant to the thrusting fullness of her breasts before returning to her face. "Perhaps you should lie down and rest. At times the faintness returns."

She cast him a bewildered glance as she stood up. He sounded remarkably knowledgeable, she thought in amusement. Perhaps in that bordello where he'd worked he had become accustomed to thinking of women as weak and persecuted dolls who fainted at the drop of a hat. Well, she was definitely not in that category.

"I'm perfectly all right now," she said firmly. "I think I'll just meet Mr. Damon outside." Yusef still looked uneasy and she wouldn't put it past him to mention that brief dizzy spell to Joel, if his protective instincts were as aroused as she thought they were. "Tell Billie not to worry if I don't come back tonight." Yusef was still frowning as she paused at the door. She smiled at him gently. "You mustn't be concerned, Yusef. Mr. Damon will take good care of me."

"Mr. Damon," he repeated thoughtfully. Then his face brightened with relief. "Yes, he is a man who would care for his own. He will watch over you."

"Right, Yusef," Kendra said lightly. "Don't worry about me. You've got your hands full just keeping an eye on Billie."

"She is one who requires much care, it is

true," he said in a gentle tone. "But you will need me now, too. I will be pleased to help you when your man cannot."

Her man. Joel and she had made no attempt to hide the affection growing between them in the last week, but she hadn't been aware that Yusef had noticed. It was ridiculous even to begin to think of Joel in terms of that primitively lovely phrase. Still, those two words caused her heart to lift joyously. She closed the door softly behind her. Her man.

Seven

Joel threw open the door to the hotel room and allowed her to precede him. He smiled when he saw the puzzled expression on Kendra's face.

"To save you the trouble of asking, let me assure you that, no, this hotel wasn't chosen by me. I made the mistake of having Billie make my reservations. Instead of the Marasef Hilton, I found myself here. She told me it would be a *sinful* waste to actually live in a country and not absorb a little of the native atmosphere." His hand moved in a mocking gesture. "Behold, the real Marasef."

"I like it," Kendra said. It was obviously not a five-star hotel, but it was clean and neat and had a simple charm that was very soothing. "But you're right, I wouldn't think it would be quite your cup of tea." She glanced at him curiously. "Why didn't you move out and go to the Hilton after you saw it?"

"I planned on doing just that, but it didn't seem worthwhile for the few days I'd be here before

I moved on to the location site." His lips twisted wryly. "There's a simplicity, a basic earthiness here that's very appealing to a man as surrounded by illusions as I am."

"Perhaps you're guilty of creating a good many of those illusions yourself," Kendra said quietly. "Your House of Rainbows doesn't appear to be the setting of a man who's very interested in maintaining a sense of reality." She opened the French doors and stepped out onto a small balcony. The view was delightful: The city, bathed in the glow of the sunset, was straight out of an Arabian nights movie.

"That's why I brought you here tonight." He was behind her, his arms encircling her waist and his lips nibbling at her ear. "There's a time when illusion has to end and reality take over. We started at the wrong end, Kendra. Everything about that first night was based on misunderstandings . . . except the knowledge that something very special happened to both of us." He turned her around in his arms; his expression was grave. "I don't think either one of us recognized it for what it was, but we both knew it was strong enough to scare us silly." His lips pressed a fairylike kiss on her temple. "But tonight there aren't going to be any cases of mistaken identity, no rainbow illusions." He kissed the tip of her nose. "I'm not going to let you have even one glass of wine. Everything is going to be honest and real and as clear as the dawn." His lips touched her own in a kiss of velvet tenderness. "And I think we're going to have the answers to some very important questions before the evening is over."

She laughed shakily. "I thought I was being brought to your lair to be seduced. Didn't anyone ever tell you that seducers aren't supposed to be so earnest in the middle of their campaigns?"

"I take my seductions very seriously, indeed," he said with a grin. He kissed her again. "But this isn't seduction; it's something very different, isn't it, Kendra?"

She felt as if those green eyes were hypnotizing her and she nodded slowly. "Yes, it's something very different, Joel."

She loved him. The knowledge was suddenly as clear as the words he'd just spoken. Why hadn't she seen that quiet golden joy for what it was before? Now it seemed impossible she hadn't recognized the signs from the beginning, since the first evening at *Illusion de l'Arc en Ciel*. The physical magic had been so potent that it overshadowed everything else, yet even then she had been aware of something else playing upon her mind and emotions. Perhaps she'd been too frightened then to admit to herself that she had been caught in the sorcerer's enchanted web. But in Sedikhan she'd discovered the sorcerer was also a man: a man who could feel pain and guilt, who could laugh at himself on occasion, who could be gentle and affectionate with those he cared for. The sorcerer could invoke a frenzy of desire, but only the man could inspire love.

"Hey, snap out of it." Joel's eyes were twinkling with amusement as he gave her a little shake. "Don't you know that a lady's not supposed to go off into a gray fog when a man's making a serious declaration? It appears I'll need to concentrate all my energies on keeping your attention tonight." His arm slipped around her waist as he propelled her through the French doors back into the room.

"I ordered dinner to be served in our room when I checked in downstairs and I want to get you fed." His glance appraised her critically. "I thought if I took the pressure off and let you rest for a week you'd put on some weight, but I don't think you've gained an ounce."

"Just because I wasn't working, doesn't mean that I let myself get out of shape," she said lightly. "I still exercised for three hours before I joined you on the set every day. In my business I can't afford the indulgence of taking a full week off."

"Oh, yes, your business." His tone was sour. "That's another thing we've got to straighten out tonight." Then, as he saw the troubled frown cross her face, he smiled. "But not right now. Now I want to tell you how beautiful you are. I want to hear you talk to me in that scratchy little whisper." He sank into the large, cushioned straight-backed chair facing the balcony and pulled her down on his lap, cradling her in his arms with infinite tenderness. "I want to hold you like this and watch the lights of Marasef go on."

Her cheek rubbed against the linen of his sport coat, and she could smell the familiar scent of soap and spice. He laughed softly and gave her a swift, affectionate hug. "Sometimes you remind me of a sensuous little kitten when you move like that against me. In the back of my mind I know how much strength and stamina there is in that slender frame, but when you're lying in my arms, I have trouble remembering it." His lips nuzzled the throbbing pulse point beneath her chin. "God, you're sweet." He drew a deep, shuddering breath. "Talk to me, sweetheart. I need something to distract me or I'll blow all my good intentions and tumble you into bed in a very unromantic fashion."

She laughed as she nestled closer. "But a very fulfilling fashion," she said teasingly, gazing up at him through her lashes. "Even if I wasn't quite myself that night, I seem to remember that you made my first experience quite a satisfactory one."

"Satisfactory?" He frowned in mock outrage. "It was a hell of a lot more than satisfactory. I'm not a satisfactory lover. I'm superb." His green eyes were suddenly dancing as his hands slid to cup her breasts. "Perhaps you need something to remind you how talented I am. Just sit still and relax, love. I'm always glad to be called upon for demonstrations."

She could feel the heat of his hands through the thin cotton of her dress, and she inhaled sharply. "I think I'm going to find it a little hard to relax," she said breathlessly. Her eyes followed his strong, sensitive hands as they moved across her, stroking her as if she were truly the senuous kitten he had described.

His breathing was as shallow as hers, Kendra noticed hazily, and she could see the jerky cadence of his heart in the hollow of his throat. "Well, at the moment there are portions of your anatomy that I'd be very disappointed to see relaxed," he said thickly, his eyes fixed on the territory his hands were arousing so expertly. His thumbs and forefingers began to roll the sensitive tips of her nipples between them and she felt a sudden flash of heat that caused her to cry out.

His green eyes were glazed a smoky emerald as they flew to her face. "Did I hurt you?" Then, as he saw the flushed languor of her face, he gave a pleased laugh that was oddly boyish. He lowered his head to kiss her lips with honeyed sweetness, his fingers plucking at her with a pressure that made her arch against him with a little moan. "Do you know what it does to me to feel you swell to fit my hands like this? To know I can make you feel the same ache that's ripping me apart?" His hands left her breasts to encircle her waist and pull her close against his arousal. "See how I'm aching for you, Kendra? Do you want me like that, too, love? I need you to want me as much as I want you," he murmured as his lips pressed a hundred frantic kisses across her throat. "It never mattered to me before. I just took what I wanted from a woman and tried to give her what she wanted. But it's different with you. I'm burning up and I want you to burn with me." His hands were running over her in a wild symphony of heat, gliding over her hips, traveling with a sensual rubbing motion over her belly and between her thighs. Then he pressed her to him with bruising strength, his face buried in the side of her neck, his body tense and vibrating with raw need. "*Burn*, Kendra; I think I'll go crazy if you don't!"

"Oh, I am burning," she gasped, her hands moving desperately over his chest and shoulders, wanting to get closer to him. Then her fingers worked with trembling urgency at his shirt. "Joel, I want to touch you." Her voice was shaking with frustration as her fingers seemed to be all fumbling thumbs. "Help me to touch you, please!"

He pushed her hands away and the white shirt was suddenly undone. She pressed her face to the hard warm muscles of his chest. She'd forgotten how deliciously sensual the springy mat of hair on his chest felt against the softness of her cheek, and how the thunder of his heart reverberated beneath her ear. Her hands moved over him in erotic slow motion, her eyes closed to isolate the pleasure she drew from the touch and sound of him. He inhaled sharply as she stroked and explored every inch of the sleek muscles, his body tensing as if her gentle voyage of discovery was almost painful. His heart, leaping beneath her sensitive fingertips, seemed to be trying to burst through the wall of his chest.

"Open your eyes and see what you're doing to me, you little devil." There was a thread of amusement under the hoarse exasperation in Joel's voice. When Kendra opened her eyes, there was a hint of that same tender humor in the curve of his lips, even though his face was flushed with passion and his eyes smoldered with the same sensual need.

"Now, if you're quite through trying to turn me into a human bonfire, I suggest we repair to the bedroom before I take you here in this chair. I don't think I can . . ." He broke off as a sharp rap sounded at the door.

Kendra lifted her head. "What's that?" she asked, startled.

Joel closed his eyes in frustration. "I believe that's the Marasef equivalent of Providence saving you from a fate worse than death." He sighed and his lids flew open. "That's got to be the dinner I ordered in a moment of sheer insanity." The knock was repeated.

"But I don't want to be saved," she protested with an impish grin. "Maybe if we don't answer, they'll go away."

Swiftly he lifted her off his lap. "No, it's just as well," he said gloomily as he stood up and buttoned his shirt. "I wanted this to be something more than a roll in the hay." He smoothed his tousled dark hair, his eyes never leaving hers, then repeated as if in incantation: "Dinner, conversation, romance. I've got to remember that. Lord, I don't know if I'm going to make it, sweetheart."

Well, who was asking him to? she thought in exasperation as she watched him cross quickly to the door and open it for the waiter. She was in just as much a fever as he, but she had none of the maddening apprehension he evidently felt about satisfying that hunger. How could either of them concentrate on food after what had almost happened such a short time ago? The man was totally unreasonable. Yet there was something very endearing about his very irrationality, Kendra thought with a poignant little tug at her heart. Somehow she doubted that Joel had ever before in his life restrained himself from taking what he wanted at a moment like that. His gift of restraint might have been terribly frustrating, but it was a lovely and touching gift all the same. She would just have to exert all her energies to show him how unnecessary that restraint was.

An enigmatic smile touched her lips as she watched the waiter deck the little table on the balcony with a white damask cloth and a crystal candleholder garlanded with white camellias. All the delicious little touches of romance, she noticed with amusement. Had Joel made a special point of ordering those as well as dinner? She felt a sudden surge of love for him so strong that it overshadowed even the desire she was experiencing. It had hurt him to let her go, yet he would suppress that aching to give her this gallant and quixotic present. With tender ruefulness she noticed the lines of strain about Joel's lips as he watched the boy transfer a large covered bowl from the serving cart to the table. Yes, she definitely had to do something to make Joel see the light.

There was still a slight smile on her face when she sat down opposite Joel and served herself some of the exotic stew from the large crockery bowl in the center of the table.

"You seem to be very well pleased with yourself," Joel said with a scowl as he lifted his glass of wine. "You evidently have a talent for reversing gears that I don't possess."

"Nope. I'm in exactly the same shape you're in," Kendra said cheerfully, picking up her fork. "I'm just hoping to convince you how idiotic this is, so we can get on to more important things." She took a bite of the stew. "You know, this is very good, but I can't quite place the sauce. It tastes rather sweet."

"They make it with dates," he said absently, his eyes narrowed on her face. "I hope you're not going to try a Tom Jones style seduction." His voice was dry. "Contrary to popular myth, I understand it's extremely bad for the digestion."

"Heavens no," she denied sweetly. "It's been done far too many times before to make such tactics anything but ludicrous." She gazed dreamily over the graceful minarets and flat-roofed houses now touched with the violet shadows of early evening. "No, I had something more in line with your ideas of keeping our relationship honest and basic."

"Indeed?" Joel's voice was cautious. "Would you mind elaborating?"

"Certainly." Kendra's gaze returned to his face and her voice was silky soft running over him, as fluidly sensual as her fingers had been such a short time before. "I just want to tell you very honestly how much I want you to do all those things to me that you did in your House of Rainbows. How I want your hands all over me as if you loved every inch of my body. How empty and aching I feel and how much I want you to fill that emptiness and soothe that ache." Her velvet-brown eyes were glowing. "And I want to tell you very basically what I'd like to do to you. How I'd like to rub my hands over your chest, then run them across your back and down . . ."

"Stop." His voice was strangled and there was a feverish flush on his cheekbones. "I think that's more basic honesty than I'm capable of hearing at the moment."

"Well, you did specify conversation."

"I didn't have such erotic subject matter in mind," he said wryly. "I was thinking more along the lines of a question and answer session. We haven't had much time this week to learn very much about each other."

She didn't agree. She felt she had learned a great deal about the complex man who was Joel Damon by watching him work. His humor was as much a part of him as the hard incisiveness, as was the vision and excitement that seemed to electrify him when a scene was coming together just the way he wanted.

"Don't look at me like that," Joel said thickly. "That's even more erotic than your idea of basic conversation." He took a quick sip of his wine. "If we're to get through this dinner, I think I'd better take the initiative."

"Oh, I'm all for initiative," she said lightly. "That's what I'm trying to tell you. Would you like me to go into detail about what I'd like you to initiate?"

"No!" he said quickly. "Your family. Tell me about your family. The personnel record said your parents were deceased but that you have a brother. What's his name? Are you close?"

Suddenly she felt as if she had been doused with ice water, and her smile faded. She didn't want to think about Casey right now. To think about Casey and her responsibilities would bring an end to the happiness that suffused her. She had known this was too ephemeral to last, but she wanted to seize as much happiness as she could tonight.

"His name is Casey. And yes, we're very close."

His eyes narrowed speculatively. "You're not very outspoken on the subject, are you? Is he older or younger than you?"

"Casey's twenty-six," she answered flatly. "You're not eating," she went on, making an effort to smile. "So much for your three-part plan. We have romance and conversation, but you've taken only a few sips of that wine."

"What does he do for a living?"

Heavens, but the man was stubborn. "It's my turn to play twenty questions," she said hurriedly. "Are your parents still living?" When she saw the sudden tightening of his face, she could have bitten her tongue. "Never mind. Maybe twenty questions isn't such a great game after all."

"You needn't be so concerned," Joel said, his mouth tight. "I gather Billie's filled you in on my charming parents." He looked down at the ruby liquid in his glass. "My dear mother is still alive and well and living in Nice. As for my father . . ." He shrugged. "At last report I believe I heard he was in Argentina. He always did find Latin *senoras* more generous than most."

"You speak as if you know him very well," Kendra said slowly. "I thought he had faded out of the picture before you were born."

"Oh, he did," Joel said. "He knew he couldn't get anymore out of a tough old bird like my grandfather, so there wasn't any use in his sticking around." His eyes were still fixed unseeingly on his glass. "But I've always been a skeptical bastard and had to be shown. I looked him up one summer when I was a junior in college. He was living in Barcelona with the wealthy widow of a vintner. I spent almost a month with them." He smiled bitterly. "My father is a very charming man and completely plausible. For that month he had me convinced that *he* was a victim who had been exploited by cold-hearted, manipulative capitalists." His laugh was self-mocking. "I actually thought he cared about me. God, I was young."

"Perhaps he did care," she said gently. "Most men have some paternal feelings."

"Do they?" His lips curved cynically. "I

wouldn't know about that. Most women I know use pregnancy as a weapon or some kind of blackmail, and most men look upon it as the final lock on the door of the cage. Only my father managed to avoid that particular bondage. A very clever man, my father, but a little impatient. When he found out my money was tied up in trusts until I was twenty-five, he gave me my walking papers. He wasn't prepared to invest that many years of charm and charisma on the marginal chance he might squeeze something more out of the Damons." Joel lifted his glass in a little toast. "But I learned a great deal in that month, even so. He gave me my final diploma in human relations."

She couldn't stand it. The emptiness in his eyes was worse than pain. No, it *was* pain and she felt it too, not in sympathy, but as an actual physical ache. The need to comfort him and soothe his pain had an almost primitive urgency.

Her voice was husky despite its deliberate lightness. "I think I've reached the end of my patience." Kendra put down her fork very carefully. "I believe I've indulged you enough. Any more would just encourage that element of arrogance I've noticed in your makeup." She pushed back her chair and stood up. "Conversation, dinner, and romance are definitely at an end." As she walked briskly to the French doors, she winked at him over her shoulder. "I'm going to be in that bed in two minutes. I'll expect you there in three."

There was a hint of tenderness in his smile. "You're a bold wanton, Kendra."

"It goes with the territory. Stuntwomen are supposed to be bold and daring. It says so in the contract I signed with you." The door closed behind her.

She wasn't feeling at all daring a few minutes later, sitting, waiting, in the double bed with only a sheet covering her nakedness. Why was she suddenly so shy? She was trembling like a virgin on her wedding night. It was as if the night at the Rainbow Keep had never happened.

"Three minutes, just as you decreed," Joel said, standing in the doorway. She noticed that he had used those minutes to remove his sport coat and unbutton his shirt. In the somber twilight of the room, his lean muscular form had a panther-like beauty that took her breath away.

He came toward her, his green eyes as jewel-bright as a panther's too. "I wouldn't dare to be even a minute late, considering what an aggressive wench you are," he drawled. "So I just covered the dinner you scorned so rudely, corked the wine, and . . ." He suddenly broke off when he was close enough to see that her velvet-brown eyes were wide with uncertainty. His lips pursed in a soundless whistle as he sat down beside her on the bed. His hand reached out gently to push a silky tress behind her ear. "Why do I suspect that the stuntwoman isn't living up to her contract?" His brow lifted inquiringly. "No brashness, no daring, sweetheart?"

She shook her head. "Stupid, isn't it?" She moistened her lips nervously. "It isn't even my first time. I'm sorry, Joel."

"Don't be." He leaned forward to kiss her so sweetly that her breath caught in her throat. "I think I like it." His hand was tracing the line of her cheekbone with a touch that was featherlight, and his look was tender. "It pleases that streak of arrogance in my makeup to know I can intimidate a tiger lady like you."

"Oh, Joel." Suddenly she flung herself into his arms and clung to him with a strength that had a touch of desperation. Oh God, she loved him so much it was exploding inside her like a volcano in full eruption. "I don't feel like a tiger lady, a rainbow lady, or any kind of lady at all. I feel like a woman who wants to be loved. Please make love to me, Joel."

"I intend to." He drew back, his breathing harsh, his face flushed with desire. "I'm holding on to my control by the skin of my teeth, but I want to tell you something first, love." His head lowered, and each word was a soft kiss against the hollow of her throat. "You've always hated my calling you rainbow lady. I guess you had a right to, considering what it meant to both of us in the beginning." He looked up and his eyes were grave. "I just wanted you to know that it doesn't mean the same thing to me now. You're still my rainbow lady, because I'll always see in you all the beauty and radiance I want in my life, but it's a radiance that's not going to fade away. Not ever, Kendra."

How could a silence say so much, mean so many shining things? Her heart was so full, it felt as if it must burst. Oh dear Lord, if only this moment could last forever, she thought.

Then Joel's eyes were no longer serious, but twinkled. "Now, like the genius I'm reputed to be, I have no intention of letting you respond to that without consolidating my position." His hands gently pushed the sheet down to her waist, baring her breasts. "Let's see how long it takes to find the pot of gold, rainbow lady."

His breath was warm, but not warm enough to ignite the streak of flame that shot through her as his lips tugged at one rosy peak. "Incredible," he murmured, his eyes dark and glazed with need. "You're so incredibly lovely you take my breath away." He blew gently on her breast, then laughed huskily as she gave him the response he wanted. "You swell like fruit ripening in the sun." He took her hand and brought it to the urgency of his arousal. "Touch me, hold me, love. I want you to know how you're making me ripen, too."

Then his lips closed tenderly on her nipple, sucking gently, then using his teeth to nibble in a caress that made her arch up to him with a little gasp. It was as if he were controlling a hot wire connected to the center of her being, and each gentle tug brought a flash of electricity that burned through her, robbing her of breath and increasing the aching emptiness between her thighs.

Joel lifted his head, his face flushed and his cheeks hollowed and taut. "God, you're driving me crazy. I want to feel *you* around me, I want your hands loving me, and your long lovely legs pulling me closer—"

"Be still," she gasped. She was trembling so badly that she could hardly get her breath. "Please, don't talk anymore. Make love to me!"

"Very soon." His breath was as labored as her own and she could see the pulse jumping wildly in his temple. "I want us to take it slowly if we can. That night at Rainbow Keep I wanted you so much I couldn't wait. I couldn't get enough of you fast enough to satisfy me."

He stood up and slipped off his shirt. He reached up and suddenly the hammered copper hanging lamp beside the bed cast a golden pool of light. "That's better. In the lamplight your hair shines as if it's on fire."

His hands worked swiftly at his belt. His supple shoulders were glowing like the copper of the lamp, and his hair was the color of midnight in the cozy circle of light that surrounded them.

"Now I'm ready to resume that little conversation we were having at dinner." He was stripping swiftly, his eyes on her face, his voice a silken murmur. "Listen carefully, sweetheart, while I tell you all the things I'm going to do to you tonight. I learned a few other things from my father, things that I enjoyed far more than that final lesson I mentioned. He knew a great deal about how to give pleasure to a woman, and it amused him to have such an eager pupil in me. I'm going to use every bit of that knowledge on you tonight." His gaze moved lingeringly down her body to the indentation of her navel, and she felt her flesh tauten and burn wherever his olive eyes touched her. "What a lovely secret place on your body. I'm going to explore that pretty hollow with my finger and then I'm going to lay my head on that soft firm belly and stroke it very slowly with my tongue. I'm going to spend a long time there tasting you, breathing in the scent of you."

Kendra moved restlessly under his gaze. It was crazy, but she could actually feel the weight of his head, the slight scratchiness of his cheek, the moist warmth of his tongue. The muscles of her stomach contracted in a yearning so intense it was almost painful. "Joel, I'm *definitely* not shy anymore. Come to bed, dammit."

"Not much longer." He smiled ruefully at her. "I'm hurting, too, love, but the pleasure will be all the keener for anticipation." He was totally nude when he sat down beside her, still not touching her with anything but his eyes and words that burned into her like a sword.

He folded back the sheet with a deliberation that caused her to tense with impatience. "You have gorgeous thighs, do you know that? Sleek and strong, yet the inner flesh is so soft and warm. I remember the feel of every muscle and tendon as they parted and then wrapped around me. But I was too impatient to just sit and look at how beautiful you are down here. I'm not impatient now, Kendra. I'm going to spread those silky thighs and just gaze at you for a long, long time. I'm going to memorize every curve and hollow."

Her face grew flushed and languorous as his words inflamed her desire. Some were as beautiful and poetic as a Kahlil Gibran verse, others as graphic and bawdy as a medieval soldier's song to his lady love. It made no difference, for it was all so arousing Kendra thought she would go insane if he didn't touch her soon.

Just when she thought she could stand no more, the words suddenly ceased. Joel drew a deep, shuddering breath and smiled at her with loving sweetness. "I hope you've been paying attention, my love, because I think it's time we translated words into action." And he slowly lowered his lips to the softness of her belly.

In the hours that followed they did everything that he'd promised, and more. They were both so aroused that every touch, every kiss, every movement was both pain and bliss. When the warm velvet length of him reached into her welcoming depths, she thought she'd go berserk. She could feel herself tightening around him as if to hold him in that most intimate of all embraces. He gave a low guttural cry and then plunged into the heart of her with stunning force.

Their search for their pot of gold took them through valleys of intimacy shadowed wine-dark with passion, to mountains that rose with endless delight. They sailed seas whose tides and currents lifted and cradled them before spinning them in a whirlpool of fiery need. It was a journey like no other she had ever taken, and when they did reach the treasure Joel had spoken of, it was no more golden than the odyssey itself.

Joel's arms were clutching her desperately, his chest laboring harshly with the force of his breathing. "Don't move," he said. "I don't want to let you go yet." His hands went to cup her buttocks and cradle her even closer to him. "I want it to go on. Why the hell can't it go on forever?"

Kendra laughed breathlessly, her arms pulling him against her. "I think if it did, we'd both risk cardiac arrest." She gasped as he suddenly flexed. "Come to think of it, it might be worth it."

Then he was rolling over to face her, their bodies still linked in a magical intimacy. "You're damn right it would." He nuzzled her throat, his hands moving to enclose her breasts. "You know, maybe you did put on an ounce or so this week. These pretty things feel heavier than I remembered."

"The bane of my life," she said, making a face. "I always gain weight there first."

"The delight of mine," he said, lowering his head to salute each pink tip lightly. "A totally enchanting bane." He cuddled her closer. "Rest, rainbow lady, we've got a long night ahead."

She nestled nearer. "Not too long," she said drowsily. "You have to be on the set at six."

"Then we'll just have to make every minute count, won't we?"

Yes, every moment must be as precious as they could make it, she thought with regret. Reality would intrude only too soon.

"Come on, love. It's time to get moving."

Kendra grumbled sleepily and tried to snuggle closer to Joel's warmth. But that warmth was no longer there, and when she realized that, her lids flicked open with a vague sense of alarm. Then she relaxed as she saw Joel across the room putting on his shoes.

He was fully dressed except for his sports jacket, though his white shirt was only partially buttoned. She sat up slowly, pulling the sheet up over her breasts and brushing the hair away from her face. "We have to leave now?"

He nodded as he stood up. "It's almost four and I want to get you back to the location by five." He crossed the room to sit down on the bed beside her. His green eyes were glowing softly as they gazed at her face. "You look like a soft silky baby just awakened from her nap."

She smothered a yawn. "A baby who would like to go back to sleep. I can't seem to keep my eyes open."

"That's not surprising. I didn't let you get much rest." He dropped a light kiss on the curve of her shoulder. "Lord, you're sweet to love. I can't get enough of you. I'll be glad when this picture is over and we can get away for a little while." His lips pulled gently at her earlobe. "I have a friend who lends me his yacht, the *Sea Breeze*, occasionally. Have you ever been to the Greek Isles, Kendra? The Greeks have a special fondness for rainbow ladies, you know. They even have a goddess of the rainbow."

"It sounds wonderful," she said dreamily. "The closest I've ever been to the Greek Isles was once when I changed planes in Athens."

"Good. Then it's settled." He gave her a quick kiss on the forehead and stood up briskly. "I should be able to wrap up *Venture* in another four days. There's only the love scene and then the rest of the stunts. We'll do the horse chase Wednesday and then I'll put you on a plane for Athens that night. I'll tie up all the loose ends and meet you there Sunday."

"Wait a minute." He was moving too fast for her. She was being swept away from wishful daydreams to cold reality with a vengeance. "I said I'd like to go, not that I could." Then something else occurred to her. "And I couldn't leave on Wednesday anyway. I still have a chance at the jeep jump." Her eyes narrowed on his face. "Or was that the intention of whisking me off to Greece, Joel?"

"I won't deny I thought it might be an excellent way of killing two birds with one stone," Joel admitted coolly. "You know it's not really worth hanging around on the odd chance that Skip will give you the jump, especially when it's not necessary."

"But it is necessary," Kendra said quietly. "And I'd love to go sailing around the Greek Isles with you, Joel, but it's just not possible right now. I only have a one-week break before I start my next job." She tried to smile. "How about a long week-end in Athens instead?"

"Are you sure you could fit it into your sched-ule?" Joel asked caustically. "Perhaps you can work me in between a skydive and driving a car off a bridge into a raging river. Or was that the last picture?"

"The one before," she said dully. It had all been so beautiful, and now Joel's words were sharp barbs tearing at that beauty. "I'm sorry I don't have the kind of freedom your usual playmates enjoy, Joel, but I have certain commitments."

"The hell you do." Joel's voice was so harsh she flinched. Then he drew a deep, weary breath. "Oh God, I wasn't going to lose my temper. I swore I was going to be very calm and reasonable about it all. But I seem to have a problem when I think about you driving off a bridge. Strange, isn't it?"

"This isn't going to get us anywhere." Kendra swung her legs to the floor, wrapping the sheet around her sarong-fashion. "If you'll give me a few minutes, I'll dress and be ready to leave as soon as I can."

"Not until we get this straightened out," he said grimly. "Why don't you admit that you're just being stubborn? There's no earthly reason for you to take another job, where you could break your neck, when I can give you anything you want."

"We've been through all that before," Kendra said. "I don't trade in that particular marketplace, Joel."

"I'm not trying to set you up as my mistress, dammit." He ran his hands distractedly through his hair. "Haven't you been listening to anything I've been saying tonight?" He spoke with an odd awkwardness. "I *care* about you. I wasn't going to bring this up right away. I was going to give you time to get used to the idea." He hesitated. "I thought we might get married before we left Greece."

"Married!" Her eyes widened in shock. She felt an explosion of joy so wild and free that it took her breath away and made her dizzy.

"I know you're not ready for it yet." There was a touch of little boy belligerence in his stance. "You've made sure I know how much you value your blasted independence. But dammit, you know that what we've got is special. It's not only sex; it's a hell of a lot more and I'm not going to let you walk away from it."

Walk away from it? She wanted to bolt toward him as if he were the only safe harbor left in a stormy world. Sweet heaven, how she wanted that. But how could she run to his arms when she still had her responsibility to Casey? She had been running from that realization since the moment she had met Joel, but now it was staring her in the face. She had no right to ask anyone else to shoulder the kind of responsibility that still loomed ahead of her. Marriage would automatically shift part of her burden to Joel, and she felt she had no right to do that, even supposing he was willing to share it with her. The wrenching agony of that knowledge was so great that for a moment she didn't think she could bear it. Kendra closed her eyes and tried to gather her strength to do what had to be done. It shouldn't be all that difficult, she thought bitterly; she was a world-class expert these days at doing what had to be done.

"Kendra?" She opened her eyes to see Joel standing before her, his eyes dark with concern. "What's wrong?"

Say the words. It would be better once the words were out and standing between them. She lifted her chin and forced herself to smile. "Nothing. Nothing at all is wrong. It's just that I'm afraid we don't agree on the need for that kind of commitment. I have no intention of marrying you, Joel. I thought you knew that." There was a flash of something in his face that made her glance away hastily. Oh no, please, let her be the only one to be hurt. She couldn't stand it if she had to bear Joel's pain, too. He hadn't said he loved her, only that they had something special. Surely he couldn't be feeling the same torment that she was. She rushed on in desperation. "It's not that I don't want to continue our relationship. Naturally, I agree that physically we couldn't be more compatible. I truly like and admire you, Joel. I'll be very happy to spend as much time with you as we can possibly manage with our separate career commitments." She steeled herself to meet his eyes with steadiness. "But anything more permanent between us is impossible." She repeated with quiet emphasis, "Completely impossible."

There was no pain in his face now, only a cynical hardness that somehow hurt her even more. "Oh yes, how could I forget your precious career commitments? You'll have to forgive me for injecting a note of sentiment into what you consider a purely physical attraction." His smile was bitter. "However, I can't say I'm flattered that you'd prefer a career of risking your neck to a lifetime with me. It's pretty hard on a man's ego."

"Joel," she started impulsively. "It's not that I . . ."

"Shut up!" The violence in his voice startled her as did the sudden flare of anger in his eyes. He drew a deep, steadying breath and enunciated very carefully. "I think it would be wise if you'd just get dressed so we can get the hell out of here. I don't seem to be accepting your rejection in a very civilized manner. Funny, you'd think I'd be a pro at it by now."

She stared at him helplessly for a long moment before she gathered the sheet around her and started toward the bathroom door. She was only halfway there when he spoke again. "As for your offer to continue our affair on your terms, I'll have to give it considerably more thought." She looked over her shoulder to see him smile in bitter self-mockery. "I'd like to tell you to go to hell, but I'd probably be safer to leave my options open. Even though I could cheerfully break your neck at the moment, I still want you so much that I'm tied in knots. Does that give your ego a lift, Kendra?"

"No!" It hurt more than she could let him know. Her lips were trembling as she tried to smile brightly. "Don't worry, they say infatuation doesn't last forever. Perhaps you'll find you were right the first time about rainbow ladies."

"It's possible." There was a sudden ripple of pain on his face, and he said wearily, "No, I'm lying. I meant every damn word I said tonight and, God help me, I still mean it." He turned away. "But you can bet I'm going to do everything I can to get over this 'infatuation.' I've learned that this particular rainbow lady can be very dangerous to me." He stood at the door. "I'll wait for you in the lobby." Then the door closed softly behind him.

Eight

The nausea came on so suddenly that Kendra barely made it to the bathroom in time. The retching seemed to go on forever. When it finally subsided, she could only lean against the basin and try to gather the strength to get back to bed.

"Kendra, are you okay?" Billie was standing at the bathroom door, her violet eyes still misty with sleep, but a look of concern was on her face. "Can I do anything for you?"

"No," Kendra murmured. "It must be something I ate. Go back to bed, Billie. I'm sorry I woke you."

"It's about time to get up anyway." Billie glanced at the window; dawn was approaching and the sky was turning from black to dull gray. "We have to be on the set in a couple of hours." She frowned anxiously. "There's no way you can do that horse chase today. I'll tell Joel he'll just have to postpone it until you're feeling better."

"No!" Kendra shook her head violently and was

instantly punished for it. The heaving this time was even worse because she had nothing left in her stomach. She heard Billie's mutterings of distress and sympathy; then, suddenly, strong comforting arms wrapped around her. But they weren't Billie's arms and she looked up dazedly to see Yusef, his hair even wilder than usual, his shirt unbuttoned and hastily shoved into his pants, and his dark eyes warm with sympathy. She seemed to be disturbing the entire household. It wasn't any wonder, the way the three of them lived on top of each other in this tiny house. "It's nothing, Yusef. I'll be all right in a moment."

He ignored her and reached up to pull the chain on the commode. He cradled her in one arm while he turned on the water in the basin and dampened a washcloth. Then he was wiping her face with the cloth, and its coolness felt heavenly on her warm forehead.

"Wonderful," she murmured.

He smiled gently. "All will be well with you soon." He picked her up as if her weight were nothing and carried her back to bed, an anxious Billie following at his heels. He set her carefully on the side of the bed and carefully straightened her cotton nightgown, brushing her hair away from her face with a touch as gentle as a mother's for an ailing child.

"Sit very still." His deep voice was soothing. "Presently the sickness will go away and I will bring you tea and toast. Next time you must call me before you get out of bed. It is very bad to move swiftly. The dizziness may come again and you might fall."

"Next time," Billie echoed worriedly. "You think it's not a temporary upset?"

Yusef shook his tousled head firmly. "No, it is

the child." He smiled gently into Kendra's face. "Is that not so?"

Kendra stared back at him numbly. After the first electrifying shock, she realized she wasn't surprised at the fact itself, merely that she'd been brought face-to-face with it. She had turned into a veritable ostrich, hiding away from reality because she couldn't cope. The signs had been there for her to see, but she'd pushed them into her subconscious and refused to think about them. "Yes, it's the child," she said slowly.

"A baby? You're pregnant?" Billie's face was alight. "That's wonderful!" She paused, her expression clouding. "Or maybe it isn't. I guess a lot of women don't feel the same way as I do about babies. Do you want the baby, Kendra?"

Trust unconventional Billie not to consider first and foremost that the baby would be illegitimate, Kendra thought affectionately. Billie's sole concern was whether or not Kendra wanted the child. And she *did* want this baby, she realized suddenly. She wanted it with a fierceness that was almost primitive. Joel's baby, she thought dreamily. Green sorcerer's eyes and glossy dark curls . . . but the child would never have his cynical smile, born of pain and disillusion. She would surround her baby with so much love, so much protection that the child would only know happiness.

"I want the baby very much, Billie," she answered quietly. "I must be totally insane. I should be absolutely frantic with worry. As if I don't have enough responsibilities to worry about now. And this is going to complicate my life even more!"

"Casey?" Billie asked gently. They'd grown so close in the past weeks that Kendra had found herself confiding in Billie without the slightest hesitancy. "I can see the problem, but these things have a way of working themselves out."

Kendra distractedly ran her hand through her hair. "Soon I won't be able to work at stunting. It would be too dangerous for the baby. I'll have to find something else to do until after the birth."

"Your man will help you," Yusef said. "Mr. Damon would not want you to worry while you carried his child."

"He's right, you know," Billie said softly. "It *is* Joel's child, Kendra?"

Kendra nodded. "Yes, it's Joel's baby." Her lips tightened. "But I'm not asking him for help. I can handle this myself." She gave Billie a fierce glance. "He's not to know about this. You're not to tell him, understand?"

Billie nodded. "I won't say anything. It's your road and your decision what byways to take. I think you know you can count on me to help in any way I can."

"Yes, I know that," Kendra said warmly.

"She should tell her man," Yusef said obstinately.

"He's not my man," Kendra answered. "And I won't have him blackmailed into thinking he has some sort of obligation to me." She had a sudden agonizing memory of Joel's cynical words when they had been talking about paternal feelings. Fatherhood was "a cage," he had said. Well, there was no way she was going to shut Joel in a cage.

"Are you sure Joel would look upon it that way?" Billie's expression was troubled. "I've been watching him with you and you'd have to be blind not to see that the man really cares."

"I'm sure," Kendra said wearily. "And he may feel something for me now, but how long would it last when he realized what kind of ropes I'd be binding him with?"

"You are wrong to do this," Yusef persisted. "A man has a right to—"

"Oh be quiet, Yusef," Billie said in exasperation. "She has rights, too." She made a face at Kendra. "Despite his place of last employment, Yusef has a very small town mentality. Not surprising when you realize he grew up in a tiny village in the middle of the desert and only recently decided to see the bright lights of the city."

"He's been very kind to me," Kendra said with a grateful smile at the frowning face of the giant Arab. "You both have. I'm just sorry to have involved you in my personal problems."

"My friends don't have personal problems," Billie said lightly. "I don't let them be that selfish. Share and share alike, I say." She grimaced at Yusef. "As for our friend here, he's probably going to drive you nuts overseeing the general state of your health for the next few days. He tells me he has seven sisters at home."

"Eight," Yusef corrected. "And fourteen nieces and nephews."

"No wonder you know so much about the care and feeding of pregnant ladies," Kendra said wryly. She was beginning to feel a little better now that the first shock and dismay had worn off. Naturally there would be problems but nothing she couldn't overcome once she set her mind to it. There must be other work she'd be able to do until she could return to stunting. She only had to find it. "I appreciate the support, but I'll be able to—"

"Handle it yourself," Billie finished for her. "I'm not so sure about that. For instance, what about that desert chase this morning? You can hardly sit up, and you still expect to make a rough ride like that?"

"I'll be okay once I've rested awhile and had some of Yusef's tea and toast."

"Kendra, you're pregnant, for heaven's sake. You can't just ignore it and keep on doing the stunts you're doing. It's too rough on you."

"I can keep it up for another month or so," Kendra said. "My mother was still working when she was four months pregnant with me. She told me so. I'll just have to be more careful in picking my jobs." She smiled. "No more rolling down hills, or falling off horses."

"What about that jeep jump?" Billie asked, her violet eyes troubled. "Won't it jar you tremendously when you land on the other side of the canyon?"

"It won't be pleasant, but if the springs are adjusted right, the impact shouldn't be all that dangerous."

"And if they're not set up right?"

"Let's just say they'd better be," Kendra answered grimly. "But don't worry; Skip will see that they are."

"Oh dear, I'm going to be scared to death until it's all over," Billie said, biting her lip. "It's going to drive me crazy standing there watching and wringing my hands. I wish I could do it for you."

"Well, you can't," Kendra said with a chuckle. "This is my show, Billie. The only thing you can do for me is make sure that Joel doesn't find out I'm pregnant and keep your fingers crossed while I'm zooming over the gorge." She grimaced. "Providing I get the jump at all. Skip promised to tell me after the chase today."

"I'll do what I can," Billie said with a sigh.

"That's all any of us can do," Kendra said, stretching out on the bed and willing herself to relax. The first pink streaks of dawn were already painting the gray sky and she didn't have much time to rid herself of this damn weakness.

Kendra bent low over the black stallion's neck,

her face almost buried in the flowing mane. She was vaguely conscious of the camera crews mounted on trucks running alongside and in back of her, but she purposely blocked them out. She was going to have to use every bit of concentration she possessed to get this ride over with in one take. It had to be one take. She didn't think she'd make it through another one.

The wind was hot and wild tearing at her wig, and the desert terrain flowed by her in a blurred golden stream. Just one more bit to do and that was directly ahead on her gallop through the canyon. A sniper attack was her signal for disengaging the stirrups, slipping to one side of the stallion, and hanging from the pommel so that she was no longer visible. An old Apache stunt but very flashy and one she had done innumerable times. There was no reason she couldn't do it this time too, and then it would all be over.

The rock beside her seemed to explode in a *rat a tat tat*. The special effects team had affixed a strip of explosives to it; when they went off, it was her signal to begin the gag. Small explosive charges in the turf erupted to simulate machine gun fire aimed at the horse and rider. Then she slipped to the side of the horse, careful to maintain her balance, while positioning her legs cautiously so she could regain the saddle with equal grace and style. It seemed an excruciatingly long time before the stone walls of the canyon were no longer flashing by her and she was once more streaking past golden sand dunes. She straightened lithely back into the saddle and once more crouched over the stallion's mane. Just another mile now and she'd reach the marker that signaled the end of the chase. Soon the horse was tearing past it and she caught a glimpse of Billie and Skip standing by a jeep at the side of the road. It was over!

She reined in the stallion, turned him, and started to walk him back toward the vehicles, her breath coming in little gasps, moisture beading her forehead. Why did it have to be so darn hot? This gag was rough enough without having such smothering heat to contend with. Joel was jumping off the back of the camera truck that had come to a halt beside the jeep, and she saw Skip cross the few yards that separated the two men. She was still too far away to hear the exchange, but Skip turned and with two fingers made a victory sign. Thank God she didn't have to do the stunt again. Joel had gotten it on one take. She felt the tension rush out of her and had to make an effort not to show how relieved she was by slumping in the saddle.

The stallion's trainer was at the black's head now, his hand on the bridle and his eyes anxiously searching Kendra's expression. "How was he, Kendra?"

"Steady as a rock. Couldn't be better, Jim," she answered. "He didn't even flick his ears when the strip went off." She dismounted, one hand patting the black's neck affectionately. "His gait was smooth as glass when I . . ." Her voice trailed off as the world spun for her. She clutched the side of the saddle for support. Then Billie was beside her, holding her firmly.

"Billie, I'm so dizzy," she whispered, her mouth dry. "Cover for me, please, I need a few minutes." She closed her eyes and breathed deeply.

"Oh, damn," Billie's low voice was full of anxiety. "I knew you shouldn't have tried this today."

Kendra opened her eyes and the ground and sky were miraculously back in their proper places. But the sight of Skip and a very grim-faced Joel striding rapidly toward them almost threw her into another tailspin. Her knees no longer felt like wet spaghetti, but still she trembled. She frantically sought an excuse for her apparent weakness.

"What the hell is wrong?" Joel's voice was hard, his eyes piercingly keen. Skip was right behind him.

"Nothing," Kendra murmured. "I just dismounted too fast and . . ."

"It's her back," Billie said hastily. "She has some ligaments that haven't healed yet that give her a problem occasionally. Shall I run back to the house and get your pills, Kendra?"

"Pills?" Skip's voice was as icy cold as his gray eyes.

Oh dear, Billie couldn't have found a worse excuse if she had tried for a hundred years. She had meant well—trying to sidetrack Joel so he wouldn't guess Kendra was pregnant—but instead she had revealed the very thing Kendra had concealed from Skip!

Skip's tone was silky soft. "What kind of pills, Kendra?"

"Darvocet-N," she answered with a resigned sigh. "One hundred milligrams." Her eyes met his steadily. "But I've only used one since I've been in Sedikhan. That was the day I hurt my back on the hill and I had the next day off. I know your rules, Skip."

"Then you know I won't tolerate anything stronger than aspirin being used by anyone on the team," Skip said in a harsh tone. "You also know that I don't hire anyone who's in such bad shape she *needs* to use them. Drugs dull your reflexes and can get you killed. Even the residue in your system could slow you down the fraction of a second that could make all the difference."

"One pill, one time," Kendra said desperately. "And you said yourself that I was doing a good job.

Do you think I could have functioned like that if I was stoned?"

"Will someone please tell me what the devil Darvocet-N is?" Joel bit out between clenched teeth.

"A painkiller," Skip answered succinctly, shaking his head in disgust. "I heard rumors that you had come back too soon from that back injury, but I couldn't believe them. Never thought you'd be so stupid, Ken."

"It wasn't stupidity; it was necessity," she answered tersely. "You know damn well why I was pressured into doing it."

"Casey?" Skip's voice was empty of sympathy. "Will it help him if you get yourself killed? That's not a valid argument and you know it!"

"You're acting as if Kendra was some kind of junkie," Billie interjected indignantly. "It was medicine, for Pete's sake."

"The result is the same despite the reason behind it," Skip answered. "Do you think I don't know what it's like? Hell, I think I'd broken every bone in my body by the time I was thirty-five. No matter how careful you are, injuries happen. It's part of the game. But I'll be damned if any of my people start off with one strike against them." Skip suddenly realized that the horse trainer was still there and gazing at them with avid curiosity. "It was a good run, Jim. I'll be using you both again." Then as the man reluctantly led the horse away, Skip turned back to Kendra. "I'm not sure I can say the same for you, Ken. I don't like having my rules flouted."

"Let me get this straight." There was soft menace in Joel's voice. "You're telling me that all the time Kendra's been working on *Venture* she's been in pain so severe she's had to use drugs to relieve it?"

"No! I told you I only used it once," Kendra protested. "I'm almost well now."

"Almost," Joel repeated, his green eyes smoldering. "You let me run you ragged for two solid weeks without saying a word when you were going through God knows what kind of pain? You've got to be some kind of masochistic idiot. Why the hell would you do something like that?"

"The reason is clear enough," Skip said sharply, acting with his usual instinctive protectiveness when one of his team was under attack. "Everyone knows Kendra's had money troubles paying for all those medical bills since her brother crashed into that wall in *Death Race* four years ago. He made the mistake of signing an insurance waiver with the production company and they held him to it. Kendra was left holding the bag." He smiled grimly. "You won't find a professional in the business who'll work for that company again. But it was too late to help Casey or Ken."

"Not everyone knew," Joel said slowly, the smolder a full-fledged flame now. "She didn't see fit to tell *me* why she was so eager to break her neck."

"Why should I?" Kendra asked defiantly. "What difference does it make why I did it? The only important thing was that it had to be done."

"It makes a difference," Joel said between clenched teeth. "You know damn well it makes a difference. I want to talk to you, Kendra. *Now.*"

"This isn't any of your concern, Joel," Kendra said curtly. "This is only between Skip and me. Stay out of it."

"The hell I will!"

Trying to ignore Joel's menacing figure, Kendra took a step toward Skip. She was relieved to find that the dizziness was almost gone now. "Okay, I wasn't entirely honest with you," she said earnestly. "You said yourself you were happy with my work. You know I worked my fanny off trying to turn in a really professional job for you. I *deserve* that jump, Skip. You know I do."

She heard a brief angry expletive from Joel, but she purposely blocked him out. She had to concentrate only on persuading Skip to give her the jump. She needed that special more desperately than ever now that her stunting would be curtailed entirely within a few months. "I'm not asking any favors. I earned that jump, Skip."

"And if I give it to you now, everyone in the business is going to wonder if I'm relaxing my own rules about drugs on the job," Skip said with flinty hardness. "It will look like an actual reward for breaking the rules. How the hell can I do that?"

"You can't do it," Joel declared. "There's no way Kendra's going to make that jump."

"Can't?" Skip drawled softly. "I told you I didn't like that word. You're trespassing on my territory, Joel. This is my decision, not yours."

"You're wrong. This is very much my territory," Joel said. "It was crazy enough to consider letting her do it before you knew she was on medication. It's totally unacceptable now. You said yourself it could mean the difference between life and death."

"But she said she had only used one pill on one occasion and there was some justification then," Skip said coolly. "And if I remember correctly, a good deal of the blame rests at your feet. You were being pretty rough on her at the time."

Joel flinched. "Do you think I don't know that? Do you think I don't realize I behaved like a bastard to her?"

"The personal games you and Kendra are playing aren't my concern," Skip said. "Except when they interfere with my prerogatives." He turned to Kendra. "You're right; you've earned the jump." His lips tightened. "And I can handle any flak I'll get from the rest of the team. I'll be damned if I'll let anyone challenge my authority here."

"You're going to let me do it?" Kendra said, her face alight with hope.

Skip nodded curtly. "You've got it." He turned away. "Come on, I'll drive you back to the location. We're going to spend the rest of the day in my trailer studying the diagram of the stunt, and then we'll go over the terrain up to the actual jump itself."

"*Damn* you, Skip." Joel's voice was so charged with anger that Kendra's eyes opened wide in shock. "If anything happens to her in that canyon tomorrow, I'll strangle you with my bare hands."

"Nothing's going to happen to her," Skip said. "I take care of my people. I'll wait for you in the jeep, Ken." Then he was striding swiftly away.

Kendra started to follow him, but she was halted by Joel's iron grip on her wrists. "I said I wanted to talk to you, Kendra. That hasn't changed." His gaze remained on Kendra's face as he said, "If you'll excuse us, Billie?"

Billie gave Kendra a helpless glance before she shrugged and started for the jeep. "If you need me, just call, Kendra."

"What does she think I'm going to do, beat you?" Joel asked in a bitter tone. "The idea has a certain merit, but at present all I'm trying to do is keep you from killing yourself. I'd think Billie would understand that."

"She does," Kendra said wearily. "She's just a little overprotective. You know how Billie loves the underdog."

"Then she should be trying to protect you from yourself and not from me." His hands tightened even more around her wrists. "That night at Rainbow Keep you hadn't had too much to drink as you let me think, had you? It was those damn pills you were taking."

"I don't really know," she answered with a shrug. "What difference does it make? It probably was a combination of the two."

"Terrific," Joel said ironically. "How stupid can you get? Don't you know you should never mix drugs and alcohol? You're lucky you didn't kill yourself."

"So it wasn't very bright of me. Why can't you just drop it? Nothing irrevocable happened as a result of the mistake I made."

"Didn't it?" His lips twisted bitterly. "I think it did." His expression became even grimmer. "Why didn't you tell me about your brother? You know I would have let you have any amount of money you needed with no strings attached. Did you think I'd exact some sort of cheap sexual blackmail if you let me help you?" There was a flicker of pain in the depths of his eyes.

She glanced away. "What did you want me to do? Should I have begged you to pity the poor hardworking stuntgirl slaving to support her disabled brother? That's too corny to be real. Too corny and too degrading. I've taken care of Casey ever since the accident and I don't need charity to care for him now. I pay my own way, Joel."

"With your blood? With your life, dammit?"

"It's my life," she said flippantly, then instantly sobered. It wasn't only her life now, it was the baby's! Oh God, she prayed silently, let her make the jump safely tomorrow.

"You won't listen, will you?" Suddenly the anger and hurt disappeared behind a mask of granite. "Well, you may not think I deserve to be given any say in your life. You've made my bit role in your future very clear. But I'm dealing myself in,

Kendra. I'm giving you an ultimatum and you'd be wise to believe that I mean it."

"An ultimatum?"

"I want you to promise not to make that jump tomorrow. I want you to let me give you the money you need for your brother and to finance your training in any other career you select. No strings attached. You don't even have to see me again if you don't choose to." As she began to shake her head, he continued harshly. "I haven't finished. Now we come to the ultimatum. If you *do* make that jump tomorrow, I'll see that you're blacklisted on every set in the film world. I think you know I have the power to do it. I'll pass the word that you're uncooperative and unreliable, and the drug rumor will do the rest. And I assure you I won't be as generous about giving you your freedom from me if you force me to do that. I'll have to find a way to make sure you're well taken care of and secure, even if it means forcing you to be my mistress."

"You wouldn't do that," Kendra whispered.

"Try me," he said, a reckless smile on his face. "I'll do whatever I have to do and take as much pleasure as I can for myself along the way. It's not the role I had in mind for you, but who knows, I might learn to enjoy playing sheik to your captive mistress. It always makes a damn good story line. Maybe it has something going for it."

"I don't think you'd find it to your taste," Kendra said, lifting her chin defiantly. "You're a little too civilized to appreciate that type of situation."

"You'd be surprised. The trappings of civilization have been gradually slipping away from me since the moment I met you. Well?"

She jerked her wrists from his hold. "You'll

have to try to do what you have to do." Without looking at him she started walking across the sand toward the jeep where Skip was waiting for her. "Just as I'm going to do what I have to do."

Nine

Joel's tall, slender body was silhouetted against the gradually brightening gray of the sky. He stood on the very edge of the precipice; the wind was sharp, whipping his clothes and lifting his dark hair. A poignant loneliness radiated from that figure and caused Billie to quicken her steps.

"Ron told me you've been out here for the last two hours," she said gently as she came abreast of him. "And that you'd spent the night setting up the shot. He sent me to tell you they're all in position at the bottom of the cliff and you're to give the word when you're ready."

He nodded, not looking at her, his eyes on the chasm that yawned before them. "It's a drop of eight hundred feet; did you know that, Billie? I had the advance crews scouting the area for days to find a drop that would get the maximum dramatic effect."

"It certainly does that," Billie said with a shiver as her gaze followed his to the shadowy, boulder-strewn floor of the valley below. "It makes me dizzy just looking at it."

"Oh yes, I have a definite talent for dramatic effect." His lips curved in bitter self-derision. "The gap had to be wide enough so that every person who had the money to fork out for a theater seat would gasp in wonder when my spunky little inge-nue miraculously soared over it to land safely on the other side. I spent hours over the storyboard planning the shot just at sunrise so the jeep would be arched against a backdrop glorious enough to be worthy of my masterpiece." He jammed his hands in the pockets of his windbreaker. "I didn't give a thought to the person who was making that jump. Don't you think that's funny, Billie?" He laughed mirthlessly. "I never even gave it a thought."

"It wasn't your job to worry about it," Billie said, her eyes fixed worriedly on Joel's face. There was an air of terrible stress about him so vibrant it was almost tangible. "You just create the concept and turn it over to the proper people to implement it."

"The proper people being one Kendra Michaels."

"She's good, Joel. She's the best in the busi-ness or she wouldn't be working on a picture with a budget the size of *Venture*. She'll make it."

"Do you know how many stunt people have been killed or seriously injured in the last ten years?" Joel asked, his eyes fixed compulsively on the jagged rocks below. "I've made a study of the subject in the past two weeks so I have all the sta-tistics at my fingertips."

"Look, Kendra's not afraid," Billie said. "She was up with Skip until after midnight going over every aspect of the jump, and she's not worried."

"But then she thinks she's Supergirl and Wonder Woman all rolled into one," Joel answered. "Most of those accidents I mentioned weren't due to lack of skill or bad timing. They were due to mechanical or technical failure of some kind. Even if she's the best driver on the face of the earth, it's not going to help. If something goes wrong with the jeep on the approach to the jump it will lack the power to gather enough momentum for spanning the gulf."

"That's not going to happen," Billie assured him staunchly. "Kendra has the utmost confidence in Skip. He wouldn't let her take the jump without triple-checking everything about the jeep. She's going to be fine, Joel. You've got to believe that."

"Yes, I've got to believe that," Joel said dully. If he didn't he wouldn't be able to survive this nightmare he had choreographed for himself. "Do you know, when I was a kid, I was always afraid to believe in anything. It seemed like everything I believed in turned out to be built of sand. From the Santa Claus myth to sweet maternal affection, it all turned out to be a bunch of crap. I couldn't believe in any of it because none of it was real. Nothing in my life's been real until now . . . until Kendra." He drew a deep, shaky breath. "So I'd better start learning how to believe, hadn't I?" The first tentative rays of sunlight suddenly brightened the sky, illuminating his face, and Billie caught her breath at the torment she saw there. "God, I've *got* to believe she's going to make it."

"Joel," Billie's hand closed impulsively on his arm. "You mustn't—"

"Come on," Joel said abruptly as he turned and started back down the road to where the rest of the crew waited at the bottom of the cliff. "We've only got fifteen minutes to get everything in position for the jump." His face was once more masked as he took her elbow and propelled her swiftly down the road. "The camera crew on the helicopter is ready to take off at a moment's notice, but the positions of the crews on either side of the canyon and at the cliff facing the chasm have to be double-checked before I give the signal." His smile was bittersweet. "I wouldn't want to lose a single angle of my fantastic sunrise backdrop, would I?"

"No, that would be a shame," Billie said absently as she half skipped to keep up with Joel's long stride. "Joel, Kendra didn't seem worried about the jump itself, but she mentioned something about the springs of the jeep being prepared properly. She was a bit grim about the importance of that. What would happen if something went wrong with the springs?"

Joel's fingers on her elbow tightened to an almost bruising force. He looked straight ahead, his eyes on the crowd of milling technicians a few hundred yards along the road. He could see the jeep now and Kendra standing beside it, listening intently to something Skip Lowden was telling her. "What would happen? She'll be going at fantastic speed and hit the other side with a tremendous impact. If the springs hold rigid instead of giving and cushioning her as they should, it will have the same effect as jumping from a ten-story building." He paused. "It would break her back, at the least."

It was almost time. Kendra felt a glowing warmth as another stuntman she scarcely knew gave her a hard hug and murmured a gruff, "Luck, Ken" in her ear. She knew it was tradition to give this physical comfort and support before a potentially dangerous gag and she'd done it many times herself, but still it touched her. Once she was in the driver's seat of the jeep, she would know only that terrible cold aloneness; even the excitement would be the icy thrill of danger. But she would have the memory of strong arms and warm words to ward off that coldness. It always helped to know that, and she would need all the help she could get today.

Joel's biting anger had shaken her more than she had let him see yesterday. She'd had to force herself to resist the impulse to give in and do anything, be anything he wanted. Yet how could she, when it meant giving up her pride and independence for what might be a fleeting liaison? Joel wanted her now. What about next year or the year after, though? She wouldn't be able to stand it if she wasn't able to teach him to love her as she loved him. And what chance would she stand with a man who had learned distrust and cynicism in the cradle?

But Lord, how hard it had been to turn and walk away from him when she wanted only to flow into his arms like a hurt and weary child. He hadn't given her so much as a word or a glance since he had stalked down from that clifftop like Moses with his tablet of commandments. Well, what had she expected but anger and rejection after the way she had deliberately tried to alienate him? She should have been prepared for the pain her actions would bring her. But she mustn't think about the hollowness she felt as she watched him move with lightning speed and sure dominance from group to group in preparation for filming. She mustn't think of anything but the jump itself.

"Ken." She pulled her glance away from Joel to find Skip once again beside her. "The mechanics and I have just completed one last check on the jeep. It couldn't be better. You're going to have a real smooth ride."

"Of course I am," Kendra said lightly. "Nothing would dare go wrong with you running the show."

"You're damn right," Skip drawled. "Keep it in mind when you're zooming over that abyss. You wouldn't want to damage my reputation by doing something stupid like smashing yourself up on those rocks." Then his rare smile appeared. "I not only expect you to make the jump, but break the existing record. Think you can handle that?"

"Sure, why not?" She knew Skip didn't give a damn about records, no matter how competitive other stuntmen were about their feats. He was just feeding her every bit of incentive he could in these last minutes. "I'll fly across the canyon as if I had wings."

"See that you do." Skip enfolded her in a brief warm hug. "See you on the other side, kid." Then he was striding swiftly away.

On the other side. That was a phrase that could be taken more than one way. She shook her head ruefully. Goodness, she was getting morbid. Perhaps it *was* time she left the really dangerous side of the business.

"The camera trucks will be ready to roll in a few minutes." It was Joel speaking beside her, his voice as impersonal as his expression. "The helicopter is taking off now and I want them to be in position to take the aerial shot before you start the run. Ron will notify you on the mobile phone when they're ready for you. I'll be with the camera crew on the other cliff when you land. Try to be ready to start the second he gives you the word. We don't want to lose that perfect sunrise backlighting, do we?"

"I'll be ready," she said, trying to smile lightly. "I wouldn't think of disappointing you by messing up the most dramatic shot in the picture. Besides, I'll enjoy the switch of driving into a sunrise instead of riding off into the sunset." She was babbling and she couldn't seem to stop. If he would only go away so that she wouldn't have to see that flinty look in his eyes, the muscle working in his jaw. "The last two pictures I did were westerns and I always seemed—"

"Be quiet." Joel's hands were heavy on her shoulders. "For heaven's sake, be quiet. After watching half the people on the set bidding you a fond farewell as if you were the star of an Irish wake, I can do without your flippant remarks."

She found his face oddly blurred and it was hard to speak over the tightness in her throat. "There was nothing funereal about it. They were just trying to give me comfort and strength in the only way they know how. I'm sorry if you don't approve."

"I didn't say I didn't approve." His voice was husky and his olive eyes oddly bright in the misty morning light. "I'm just jealous as hell you need anyone else but me. I want to be the only one you turn to for help."

He drew her into his arms carefully, as if she were very fragile and might break at the slightest touch. His cheek was hard and cold against her own, but his lashes pressed against her temple were warm and moist. Moist?

"Take from me, rainbow lady. Use me. I want to give you all the strength and skill you need to get across that canyon." He was rocking her with the most exquisite tenderness she had ever known. "Oh God, I feel as if I could lift you over it myself by sheer force of will. Know that, Kendra. Know that I'll be willing you across that damned abyss with everything that's in me." He kissed her with desperation and ferocity. "You've got to make it, dammit!" Then he released her and strode quickly toward the camera truck. He didn't look at her again as he jumped in the back and shouted "Let's go" to the driver.

Kendra drew a deep breath, feeling a little dazed as she watched the truck turn and race down the road to the canyon floor. Dazed and yet she was experiencing an inner fire that seemed to warm every atom of her being, banishing the cold, banishing the fear she wouldn't admit even to herself. Perhaps Joel really was the sorcerer she had thought him that first night. She could almost believe he could lift her over the canyon by will alone. By will . . . or was it something else? The question brought such a wild soaring hope she found herself trembling. No, she mustn't start to think of that possibility now when all her concentration must be on the job.

She turned and climbed into the driver's seat of the jeep, fastening the special seat belt before leaning back in the seat and closing her eyes. She cleared her mind of everything but what lay ahead of her, mentally going over the route and focusing on the point where she must gun the accelerator to gain enough momentum to make the jump. She forced herself to relax the tense muscles of her neck and shoulders. Hang loose. In a few minutes it would all be over and she'd be zooming over the chasm. She wouldn't be alone for long. She'd be able to see Joel and the camera crew even as she made the jump. She would see him on the truck and know that he was making his own special magic and willing her to come to him. Then she'd be landing on the other side of the canyon where Joel was waiting. Where love was waiting.

She heard the crackle from the mobile phone—Ron from the helicopter with the signal for her to start. She opened her eyes and turned on the ignition of the jeep before reaching with a steady hand for the receiver to tell him she was ready.

* * *

The film sequence of the jeep soaring over the canyon won the camera crew on the helicopter an Oscar nomination. It was unforgettable: a small, black car silhouetted against the glory of the scarlet sunrise. The valiant sturdiness of the small jeep and the fragile figure of the woman at the wheel pitting their strength against the emptiness that yawned below caused the heart of a viewer to leap. It wasn't only the sheer marvel of the feat that created such excitement, but also the incredible beauty of the concept itself.

To Joel, watching Kendra hurl herself into nothingness from the other side of the canyon, it seemed as if the jeep were suspended in midair for centuries instead of seconds before it began its descent. Then it moved in ultra slow motion until it hovered over the safety of the cliff. Suddenly the air was rent with violent sound and spewing of earth as the wheels of the jeep landed in a bone-jarring crash and skidded for an eternity before coming to a halt less than a hundred yards from where the cameras were set up near the truck.

He dimly heard the roar that went up from the crew and felt Billie grab his arm and squeeze it in a rapture of relief and delight. But he saw only the slim delicate woman in the driver's seat, the copper curls of her wig bright in the sunlight as she bent forward. What was she staring at so intently? Then he realized her body slumped oddly.

"Oh God, no," he breathed, and it was a prayer. Then he was running toward the jeep, forgetting the cameras that were still rolling. *"No!"*

Her lashes were dark shadows on her cheeks and her lips were parted like those of a sleeping child. She was so still that at first he thought she wasn't even breathing, and it caused an icy panic to grip him as he fumbled frantically at the seat belt holding her prisoner. Suddenly he found his shoulders gripped by a steely hand, yanking him backward.

"Don't touch her." Skip Lowden's voice was an urgent growl. "Haven't you got any sense at all, Damon? I've radioed down to the first aid tent for them to send up a van and a medical team. They'll be here within ten minutes."

"She's hurt!" Joel's eyes were blazing as he turned to face him. "You were so sure nothing could happen to *your* people. That all your cross-checks would keep her safe. She trusted you. And you may have killed her, damn you!"

"She's not dead," Skip said, his finger on the pulse point on Kendra's throat. "But she's unconscious and that means some type of injury. We can't move her until we find out just exactly what we're up against. I've got to look at the springs to make sure something didn't go wrong." He was already examining the seat with razor-sharp eyes. "Nothing. It should have given her a perfect cushion." His forehead knotted in puzzlement. "What the hell could have happened to her?"

"I'm not going to stand here while you worry about your blasted technical problems," Joel said through clenched teeth. "Is her back broken or not?"

"No, there's no reason to believe there should be any broken bones from the impact," Skip said absently. "And she didn't hit her head when she landed. I don't know what the hell is wrong with her."

"Oh for pity's sake, are you two just going to leave her in that seat while you try to diagnose what's the matter with her?" Billie's voice was seething with exasperation as she pushed between them and bent over Kendra. "Let's get her out of here. If there aren't any bones broken, there shouldn't be any danger. She looks wretchedly uncomfortable."

Skip frowned. "I don't know if—"

"There's nothing seriously wrong," Billie said crossly. "Can't you see, she's just fainted."

"If she's fainted, then there must be a reason," Skip said stubbornly. "We'll have to wait for the medical team to take her down for X rays. There's a portable unit at the first aid tent."

"X rays!" Billie's eyes widened. "They can't do that. I told you there's nothing wrong with her."

"They'll have to make sure," Skip said with a shrug. "We can't take the chance."

"They can't do it!" Billie interrupted violently. "X rays might hurt the baby!" Billie took one look at the stunned faces of the two men facing her and closed her eyes. "Oh Lord, now I've done it. I promised I wouldn't say anything about her being pregnant."

"*Pregnant.*" Joel repeated the word dazedly. He shook his head to clear it. Kendra pregnant. Kendra carrying his child. It was too much to comprehend after the panic that had gone before. "You're sure, Billie?"

"I'm sure," she said gloomily. "Kendra didn't want anyone to know. She's probably going to kill me." Her chin lifted belligerently. "Now that you know what's wrong with her, can we please get her to the first aid tent? I'm not sure all that jarring wasn't harmful for her and the baby."

That chill of panic returned and Joel shook his head. "We'll still wait for the paramedics. I'm not going to risk hurting her." She was too deeply unconscious for his peace of mind and Billie was right about that bone-jarring impact. God, he didn't know anything about pregnancy. For all he knew it could be as dangerous for Kendra as that damn jump she had just made across the canyon. What if she was bleeding internally or something?

"Radio to Marasef," he ordered Skip. "I want the best doctor in the city waiting at the first aid tent when they get her back down there." With a surge of relief he saw the van racing up the road and started forward to meet it, with Billie following in his wake.

Ten

The bedroom was dark except for the soft diffused light streaming through the amber beads of
the door when Kendra opened her eyes. For a
moment in the haze of first awakening it was so
like the many other times she'd awakened in this
room that she half expected to hear the chords of a
guitar and Billie's voice softly singing in the other
room. But there was no sound except the light
rhythmic breathing coming from the other couch
against the wall. Billie, she thought drowsily, her
gaze wandering to the couch. But the head on the
cushions wasn't copper but raven dark, and the
shadowy figure definitely masculine. Joel!

The realization shocked her wide-awake and
she sat bolt upright in the bed as a torrent of memories and emotions rushed back to her. The jump,
that moment of explosive triumph when she had
hit the other side, the sudden dizziness and
threatening darkness. She'd scarcely had time to
turn off the ignition before that darkness had

closed on her. It was evident some time had passed since it was obviously night, but why was Joel in that other bed instead of Billie?

The baby! Had the jarring impact hurt the baby? No, there had been no pain, just that same dizziness she'd known before. The baby was safe, thank heavens. And now that the jump was over, she'd be sure she kept him safe. No more driving off bridges and jumping cliffs while she had him tucked under her heart.

She heard Joel stir in the next bed and it brought her abruptly back to the present. That exquisitely poignant moment in Joel's arms before the jump had filled her with hope and given her the strength she had needed so desperately. In retrospect, however, she couldn't understand the joy she'd known. Surely the situation would be just that much worse if Joel did love her. She still couldn't impose her obligations on anyone else, much less someone she loved as much as Joel. But how could she face him and say the words of rejection again? She'd done it once and it had almost torn the heart from her. She couldn't go through it again, even if it meant running away from a confrontation before Joel awoke.

She silently swung her legs to the floor and stood up. She moved with catlike softness across the room to the closet. Carefully holding the beaded strands so they wouldn't click, she grabbed jeans, a beige shirt, tennis shoes, and her purse. Then she was gliding toward the door. More beads, she thought crossly. Billie's "atmosphere" was all very well, but clangy as the devil. Joel must have been sleeping very deeply, though, for he didn't stir when she passed through the door. There was no sign of Yusef or his bedroll, she noticed, as she dropped her bundle of clothing on one of the wooden kitchen chairs. Where was everybody?

Well, she'd just have to worry about that later. Her first priority was getting dressed and away before Joel awoke. Which wasn't going to be all that easy considering how weak and sluggish she was feeling.

She almost made it. She had just finished tying her tennis shoes, had stood up, and was reaching for her shoulder bag on the table when she heard Joel's caustic voice behind her. "What's the hurry? Do you have another canyon to jump before dawn or do you always do flits in the middle of the night?"

She stiffened and drew a deep breath before turning to face him. He was standing in the doorway dressed in black jeans and a black cotton shirt with the sleeves rolled to the elbow. His hair was rumpled and there was a dark shadow of growth on his hollow cheeks that made him look faintly rakish. "I just thought it was time to get up," she said brightly. "I must have been more tired than I thought to pass out like that." She moistened her lips nervously. "I assure you I don't usually sleep from sunrise to sunset. Was the take this morning okay?"

"I haven't the slightest idea," Joel said as he came toward her. "I haven't been out of this house since we brought you down from the canyon after the jump." He paused. "And it's considerably later than sunset. It's almost two in the morning."

"Two!" she echoed, her eyes widening. She couldn't have lost that much time. "That's not possible. I wasn't that tired."

"Weren't you?" He was coming toward her, his expression grim. "According to the doctor who examined you when I brought you back from the canyon, you were suffering from exhaustion, a slight case of anemia, and those tendons in your back may give you trouble for the rest of your life if you don't stop abusing them. It's no wonder you collapsed."

"You had a doctor examine me?" She felt a swift rush of panic. "You had no right to do that without my consent."

"And you would never have given me that consent, would you, Kendra?" He was close enough so she could see the lines of weariness that were etched in his face and the mauve shadows beneath his eyes. "Because you knew what else the doctor would tell me and you didn't want that at any cost. You didn't want me to know about my baby, did you?"

She inhaled sharply, her knees suddenly weak. "Your baby?" she asked, lifting her chin proudly. "It's not your baby, it's mine, Joel. It's my responsibility and I'm not about to involve you. You're right, I wasn't going to tell you, because it's my concern and not yours."

"Not my concern?" He shook his head incredulously. "What the hell are you talking about? I put *my* seed in your body and it will be my child that will be growing in your womb."

His hand reached out and touched her belly and rested there. She could feel the heavy warmth through her jeans as he rubbed her gently. "It's my baby in there now, the baby we made together. You can't say that I'm not involved." His eyes narrowed. "Or are you trying to tell me I'm not the father?" He shook his head. "No way, sweetheart. I won't buy it."

"No, it's your child," she admitted wearily. "But that doesn't change anything. The night of conception had to be at *Illusion de l'Arc en Ciel*, and you certainly didn't force yourself on me. Why should you be held liable for making love to a woman you assumed was willing and capable of protecting herself?" Her lips tightened stubbornly.

"Don't worry about me, Joel. The whole thing was my fault and I'll assume the responsibility. I don't expect anything from you."

"Do you think I don't know that?" His voice was suddenly fierce. "You don't expect anything; you won't accept anything. You're so damn independent that you'd rather lose the baby than let me carry my share of the responsibility."

"No, that's not true," she gasped. "The baby won't be harmed; I'll see to that. I'll rest more and I'll take iron tablets and—"

"Kendra, for God's sake, I can't take any more." His green eyes were full of torment as he took her shoulders in his hands and looked down at her. "Do you know the hell you're putting me through? How the devil can you be so damn selfish?"

"Selfish?" Kendra echoed, bewildered. "I'm not asking anything of you."

"That's the whole point," Joel said. "Do you know how much I want to give to you? All my life I've been afraid of giving a part of myself and so I've stood on the outside looking in at life." His hands were moving caressingly on her shoulders. "I'm not afraid anymore, Kendra. I don't care if you don't feel the same way as I do. All I want is for you to stay with me and let me love you. I'll take a chance on the rest. Just let me love you and give to you." He pulled her close and held her with a gentleness that was exquisitely tender. "I have a whole lifetime of loving and giving saved up. Please, don't shut me out, sweetheart."

Her hand clutched at his shirt as she buried her face in his shoulder. "It's not fair," she whispered, her throat tight and aching with tears. "You said you didn't have any paternal feelings. I won't have you caught in that cage you mentioned."

She felt his chest move beneath her ear as he

chuckled. "I said most men didn't have them, not that I personally didn't. I want our child very much, love. In the past eighteen hours while you've been snoozing so peacefully I've been thinking a lot about that." His lips touched her temple. "In fact, I've grown quite primitively possessive about the little tyke. For heaven's sake, woman, you ought to know I didn't have any qualms about your becoming pregnant after that night at the hotel."

"But that was the night you told me—"

"You should have believed the adage about actions speaking louder than words," he interrupted. "Didn't it occur to you that if I didn't want you pregnant, I would have used some protection that night? You're green as grass, sweetheart, and I was feeling guilty as hell about taking advantage of that naiveté." His arms tightened about her possessively. "I promised the next time I'd protect you and I broke that promise. I was so desperate I was willing to try every dirty trick in the book, even getting you pregnant."

"You wanted me to become pregnant?" She leaned back in his arms to look up at him with startled eyes.

"I wanted you any way I could get you," he said quietly. "I've never loved any woman before and I'll never love another one as long as I live. I know how lonely it gets out there in the world without someone to love and I don't think I could go back to that now." He leaned forward to kiss her forehead gently. "Not now, rainbow lady."

"Joel." He was breaking her heart into a million pieces. He hadn't even asked if she loved him, only assumed that she didn't. How many years of rejection and pain had ingrained that wariness in him? Yet he was willing to yield her his love without even asking for any return commitment. Two tears that had been brimming suddenly rolled down her cheeks. "Joel, I've no right to ask you to assume my problems. Casey has no claim on you even if you think your child does." She met his gaze steadily. "I can't relinquish my responsibility to him as long as he needs me and I don't even know how long that will be."

His eyes were grave as her own. "My rainbow lady wouldn't know how to turn her back on someone who needed her, I know that," he said softly. "That's why I'm counting on her to make room in her heart for me. For there's no one on the face of the earth who needs her more than I do."

"But Casey—"

"Casey is your brother and if you find him worthy of love, then I will, too," he said. "You'll have to help me out now and then with this love business. I'm a novice at the game." His voice deepened. "But if you'll stay with me, I'll learn to love the whole darn world if that's what you want."

She felt as if her heart and soul were melting into a river of gold that wanted to flow around him, surrounding him with warmth and love and everything he wanted in this life and the next.

"Now, who's being selfish?" she asked tenderly, her eyes glowing with a light that was almost incandescent. "You just told me how important giving is to you and you're practically drowning me with your generosity. Don't you think you should give me the opportunity to give as well?"

He was still. "I told you I'd take whatever I could get," he said slowly. "What do you want to give me, Kendra?"

Her index finger reached up to trace gently the hollow of his cheekbone. "Suppose we start out with my body and my spirit," she said, smiling at him so lovingly it took his breath away. "Then we'll work up to passion, devotion, laughter, and top it off with so much love that I may smother you. Do you think you can handle that, Joel? Will you let me give you all of that for the rest of my life?"

"Oh yes, I can handle that." His eyes were bright as he bent his head slowly until their lips were only a breath apart. "You're sure, Kendra? You don't have to pretend to feel something for me if you really don't. It's enough to know that you'll stay with me. I'd rather you were honest with me in the beginning. I don't think I could take it if I believed you and then found out it wasn't true."

"I'm sure." The tears were falling and she couldn't seem to halt them. How many years would it take her to convince him that he was loved and that that love wasn't an illusion which would vanish as the others had in his life? Well, it didn't really matter. They had all the rest of their lives and it would come in time. Her lips parted and took his in a kiss that wove all the shades of loving and tenderness about him. "Just give me a chance, and I'll show you it's true."

His arms closed around her with a desperation that took her breath away. "I'll give you all the chance you need," he said huskily. "But don't ever try to walk away from me, love. I'll never let you go. I couldn't live without you now."

She laughed shakily, "Who's walking?" The atmosphere was too emotion-charged to be borne, and so she teased him. "I couldn't if I wanted to with this bodylock you've got me in. I'm enjoying it excessively, but do you suppose I could take an occasional breath?"

"Oh God, am I hurting you?" He released her so swiftly that she almost fell. "I forgot about your back." A frown darkened his face. "You shouldn't even be on your feet, for heaven's sake. Why the devil couldn't you stay in bed and rest like you're supposed to do? The doctor said you should have bedrest for at least a week and take it easy for the duration of your pregnancy." He sat down in the wooden upright chair and pulled her down in his lap. "Rest, dammit."

"Yes, sir," she said meekly, leaning back in his arms with a sigh of delicious contentment. "Whatever you say. I always try to be cooperative with my directors, whenever possible."

She felt him stiffen against her. "Yes, I've noticed how cooperative you are." There was a tinge of bitterness in his tone. "You tumble out of airplanes and jump across canyons at the lift of an eyebrow." Then as her eyes flew swiftly to his face, he drew a deep breath and spoke wearily. "Sorry. I wasn't going to say anything like that again. That's another thing I made up my mind about while you were sleeping. If you'll wait until after the baby's born and you've fully regained your health, I won't fight you if you want to go back to stunting."

"You mean that?"

"I mean it. It's going to tear me to pieces every time you do one, but I'll learn to live with it."

"That's very generous of you." It was more generous than she could have been under the same circumstances, Kendra realized. She wouldn't have been able to bear standing by while Joel took risks that might maim or kill him. It would be a living nightmare that made her shiver just to think about it.

"I don't feel generous. I feel damn savage." His lips twisted. "But if it's important to you, I don't have any choice. I can't risk making you so unhappy that you'd want to leave me."

"And there's nothing important enough that I'd risk hurting you," she said softly. "Stunting is a job to me. It's all I've ever known, but it's not a profession I can't live without." Her eyes were thoughtful. "I don't think I'd ever be content without some kind of work to do, so don't expect me to sit home in domestic bliss."

She could feel the tautness seep out of his muscles, and his smile was a flash of sunlight so brilliant it would have melted a glacier. "Oh God, sweetheart, you can become a lady wrestler or a brain surgeon, just as long as you're not driving off bridges."

She grinned impishly. "I don't think either one of those professions would appeal to me, but I'll take them under consideration. They'd both require a great deal of physical stamina and my training would certainly stand me in good stead." She nestled her head on his shoulder. "No, I was thinking more on the lines of camera work or set dressing so I could tag along and keep an eye on you." Her lips brushed the throbbing pulse of his throat. "I want to be a part of every aspect of your life, Joel. I'm not about to be shut up like some fairy-tale princess at *Illusion de l'Arc en Ciel* when I can be with you in the real world. I told you I was a very pragmatic lady."

"So you did." His hand tangled in her hair as he pulled her head back. He kissed her with a passionate sweetness that had them both breathless and glowing when their lips parted. "Have I ever told you that I love pragmatic ladies almost as much as rainbow ladies?" He gave her a light kiss on the end of the nose. "And now I think I'd better display how pragmatic I can be myself and hustle you back to bed." His eyes narrowed thoughtfully. "I'll call Jake and ask him to send the *Sea Breeze* to Athens right away. It's docked in Miami right now, so it should arrive there by next week. That will give me time to finish tying up loose ends here and let you get in that week in bed the doctor ordered."

"I'm not staying in bed for a week," Kendra

said crossly. "I'll be perfectly all right by tomorrow. I'd go crazy lounging around like some kind of fragile flower."

"And I'd go crazy worrying about you if you didn't." His lips tightened. "You'll stay in that bed if I have to tie you down hand and foot." Suddenly his eyes began to twinkle. "Perhaps that wouldn't be such a good idea after all. That brings a very lascivious picture to mind and I doubt if you'd get much rest if you unleashed all my kinky fantasies."

"Then I'd be better off trailing after you, wouldn't I?" Kendra asked pomptly. "Don't worry, I won't get in your way." She let her eyes widen wistfully and her lower lip tremble slightly. "Unless you don't want me."

"Knock it off, Kendra," Joel growled. "You know that's not the issue. Look, I really need to get this picture wrapped up, but if it's a case of sitting on you to get you to stay in bed, I'll do it. You'll just make my work that much harder."

"That's a low blow," she said gloomily. "Okay, I guess I'll just have to resign myself to being a lady of leisure for the next week. I'll find *something* to occupy myself." Her brow knotted thoughtfully. "Maybe I can talk Billie into teaching me how to play the guitar." Suddenly her eyes flew to his face. "Where are Billie and Yusef anyway?"

"At the present, they're probably camping out in the wilds of nowhere," Joel answered. "She only stayed long enough to make sure you were fine, and then she and Yusef took off in the jeep into the desert." He scowled. "I tried to talk her out of it, but it was like talking to the wind." He shifted and reached into the back pocket of his jeans and pulled out a rather creased envelope. "She left a note for you."

The note was typically Billie.

Kendra,

I think you're wrong about Joel and I have an idea you're going to find that out for yourself very soon. If you decide that your path lies with him—be happy. If not, why don't you try another road and see what's around that next corner? There's a big wonderful world out there just waiting for you.

Either way, I thought you'd feel more comfortable if you were able to maintain your independence, so I instructed payroll to forward that sinfully extravagant salary Joel paid me for *Venture* to your brother's nursing home. There should be enough to clear up the bills and provide for the schooling you mentioned. Don't argue. What would I do with all that money? It would only weigh me down.

I've got to get Yusef settled before I leave Sedikhan and I don't believe he'd really be happy in Marasef. I think he's homesick for that little desert village and very disillusioned with the bright lights. I'm going to see if I can't wean him away from his allegiance to me and into a more appropriate lifestyle. Besides, he tells me his village is located near a mysterious walled city called Zalandan. Do you know what Zalandan means? Horizon! Now how could a gypsy like me resist a lure like that?

Love,
Billie

Kendra handed the note to Joel to read, blinking rapidly to keep back the tears. Sweet, crazy Billie, wanting to set the whole world right. "I can't take it, of course, but what a wonderfully generous thing to do."

"Knowing Billie, you may not have any choice." Joel looked up from scanning the note with a rueful grin. "She probably has her little trust set up so that you have nothing to say about it. Billie can be remarkably determined when she's off to the rescue. We'll just have to see what we can do." He tossed the note on the table. "But that's tomorrow. Tonight I'm going to tuck you into bed so that you can get some rest."

"For heaven's sake, I just woke up from a siesta that should prove I'm Rip Van Winkle's second cousin. How do you expect me to go back to sleep?"

"You have a point," Joel conceded as he stood up with her in his arms. "We'll just have to think of something to while away the hours until you get drowsy again." He was carrying her toward the bedroom and looked down at her with mock sternness when she chuckled. "And don't think you're going to seduce me into letting you have your way with me, you lustful woman. That wasn't what I had in mind at all." He muttered a curse as he had to fight his way through the beads, and she giggled again. "It's not funny. I could have strangled myself with those blasted beads. I'm moving you into the trailer first thing tomorrow." He laid her carefully on her bed before lying down beside her and gathering her back into his arms. "Besides, these beds aren't nearly wide enough for both of us."

She cuddled closer to his dear warmth, snuggling her cheek into the curve of his shoulder. "I like it like this; it's cozier. And since you won't let me seduce you—"

"I assure you that's not going to be a permanent state of affairs." He dusted a gossamer kiss on the top of her head. "I don't have much faith in my powers of resistance where you're concerned, love."

"Well, what *did* you have in mind then?"

His voice was deep and husky beneath her ear. "I thought I'd hold you like this all through the night and talk about dreams and unicorns and rainbows." His arms tightened around her. "Then I thought we'd speak about love and marriage and our child growing within you. I want to weave the fantasy and reality together and make them both our own. Okay, rainbow lady?"

The reality and the fantasy. Yes, it was important that the contrasting elements that made up their lives be merged, so that they could have it all. "I'd like that," she said softly, her heart full to overflowing with the reality of love and her mind full of the dreams that were the gift of that love. "By all means, let's talk about rainbows."

And she nestled closer to the sorcerer who was also a man as they began to weave the tapestry of the years to come.

THE EDITOR'S CORNER

There is a very special treat in store for you next month from Bantam Books. Although not a LOVESWEPT, I simply must tell you about Celeste DeBlasis's magnificent hardcover novel **WILD SWAN**. Celeste has demonstrated to us all what a superb storyteller and gifted writer she is in such works as **THE PROUD BREED** and **THE TIGER'S WOMAN**. So, you can imagine with what relish I approached the reading of the galleys of her latest novel one weekend not too long ago. I couldn't put **WILD SWAN** down. I wrapped myself in this touching, exciting, involving story and was darned sorry when I'd finished that last paragraph. I'll bet you, too, will find this epic tale riveting. Spanning decades and sweeping from England's West Country during the years of the Napoleonic Wars to the beautiful but trouble-shadowed countryside of Maryland, **WILD SWAN** is a fascinating story centered around an unforgettable heroine, Alexandria Thiane. And the very heart of the work is an exploration of love in its many facets—passionate, enduring, transcendent. **WILD SWAN** is a grand story, by a grand writer. Do remember to ask your bookseller for this novel; I really don't think you'll want to wait until it comes out in paperback!

And now to the LOVESWEPTS you can look forward to reading next month.

In **TOUCH THE HORIZON** (LOVESWEPT #59) Iris Johansen gives us the tender story of Billie Callahan, the touching young madcap introduced last month in **CAPTURE THE RAINBOW.** On her own at last in the mysterious desert land of Sedikhan, Billie is driving her jeep toward a walled city when she is rescued from a terrifying sandstorm by a dashing figure on a black stallion. He sweeps her into his arms and steals

(continued)

her heart. Shades of the Arabian Nights! Those of you who've read many of Iris's books in the past will recognize some old friends and thrill to the golden-haired, blue-eyed hero whose kisses send Billie spinning off the edge of the world. This lively adventure tale may be Iris's most wonderful love story to date! Don't be too frustrated now that I haven't given you the hero's name. It's a surprise from Iris. And do let me tantalize you with just a few words: he's a poignant character introduced in an early work and through letters I know many of you have complimented Iris on his creation, rooted for him, taken him into your hearts. At the end of Chapter One, you'll know his name and, I suspect, you'll be cheering!

One of the pleasures of publishing LOVESWEPT romances is discovering talented new writers, wonderful storytellers who bring us their unique insights into the special relationships between men and women. This month we're introducing two of our most exciting new discoveries: first, BJ James, whose novel **WHEN YOU SPEAK LOVE** (LOVESWEPT #60) offers an intense, dramatic and touching romance with a truly endearing cast of characters. While it was heartbreaking tragedy that brought Jake Caldwell and Kelly O'Brian together, what followed was the nurturing of a special kind of love between two people who've longed for closeness but have never known its intimate joy. We think you'll agree that BJ's first novel for LOVESWEPT is beautifully and sensitively written, a truly memorable debut.

Our second "debutante" brings a delicious sense of humor to her first LOVESWEPT romance. Joan Elliott Pickart may be **BREAKING ALL THE RULES** (LOVE-SWEPT #61) in this irresistible confection, but you'll be delighted to join in the fun! Blaze Holland and Taylor Shay both vowed they weren't looking to fall in love that wintry day in New York City, but the stormy weather wasn't the only thing beyond their control. Blaze is one of the most unforgettable heroines we've seen in a long time—and Taylor the perfect foil for her headlong tumble into the arms of love. These two give a new romantic flavor to the notion of popcorn as a potential aphrodisiac! Was falling in love always this much fun?

When you're looking for someone very special, what's the fastest way to find him? If you're Pepper, the resourceful and constantly astonishing heroine of **PEPPER'S WAY** (LOVESWEPT #62), you place an innocently provocative ad in your local newspaper that's sure to compel the perfect candidate to respond! Kay Hooper has done it again with this beguiling and whimsical tale of loving pursuit. Thor Spicer answers the ad and suddenly finds himself the object of Pepper's tireless fascination. He's never met a dynamo like this lady before, and his goose is definitely cooked! **PEPPER'S WAY** is a delightfully romantic story, brimming with the unpredictable twists and turns you've come to relish in each new book by Kay Hooper. Perhaps I shouldn't reveal this, but I've always fantasized about having certain of the unusual talents that Pepper reveals to Thor and his friend Cody in this absolutely wonderful love story!

Whew! September positively sizzles with romance that won't fade at summer's end. It's great to know you'll be there to share it with us as the leaves turn those glorious shades of red and gold!

With warm good wishes,
Sincerely,

Carolyn Nichols

Carolyn Nichols
   Editor
LOVESWEPT
Bantam Books, Inc.
666 Fifth Avenue
New York, NY 10103

WILD SWAN

Celeste De Blasis

Author of THE PROUD BREED

Spanning decades and sweeping from England's West Country in the years of the Napoleonic Wars to the beauty of Maryland's horse country—a golden land shadowed by slavery and soon to be ravaged by war—here is a novel richly spun of authentically detailed history and sumptuous romance, a rewarding woman's story in the grand tradition of A WOMAN OF SUBSTANCE. WILD SWAN is the story of Alexandria Thaine, youngest and unwanted child of a bitter mother and distant father—suddenly summoned home to care for her dead sister's children. Alexandria—for whom the brief joys of childhood are swiftly forgotten . . . and the bright fire of passion nearly extinguished.

Buy WILD SWAN, on sale in hardcover August 15, 1984, wherever Bantam Books are sold, or use the handy coupon below for ordering:

SPECIAL
MONEY SAVING
OFFER

Now you can have an up-to-date listing of Bantam's hundreds of titles plus take advantage of our unique and exciting bonus book offer. A special offer which gives you the opportunity to purchase a Bantam book for only 50¢. Here's how!

By ordering any five books at the regular price per order, you can also choose any other single book listed (up to a $4.95 value) for just 50¢. Some restrictions do apply, but for further details why not send for Bantam's listing of titles today!

Just send us your name and address plus 50¢ to defray the postage and handling costs.